Talks
to
Things

Talks to Things
By Dominic R. Villari

Published by
Figment Press
www.figmentpress.com

Copyright © 2018 by Dominic R. Villari

ISBN: 978-0-9814940-3-6

PART 1

1

"Albert…buzz…Albert…buzz…Time to get up, Albert…buzz…It's time to get up, Albert."

Albert looked over at the alarm clock on the nightstand. "Good morning," it said. He leaned over and clicked the stop button on the top of the clock.

Albert got out of bed and began his morning routine. After showering, shaving and brushing his teeth he walked back to the nightstand to collect his things.

"Busy day?" asked the reading glasses as he picked them up.

"Not too busy," replied Albert.

"Then we should take a drive," suggested the car keys as he placed them in his pocket.

"I have some errands later," said Albert.

"Let's stick to our list this time," said the wallet as Albert opened it to check the contents.

"I just need a few items," said Albert. He adjusted his reading glasses and looked down at his cell phone. There were no messages.

"Should we call someone?" asked the phone.

"Certainly not this early," said Albert. "I don't think there's anyone we need to talk to anyway." Albert went downstairs to start breakfast.

He turned on the stove and got out a pan. "What are we having today?" asked the stove.

"Eggs," replied Albert. "And bacon," he added under his breath.

"You'll need a second burner for that," said the stove.

Albert sighed. "It's microwave bacon," he said.

"Very disappointing, Albert," said the stove. "It wouldn't take you that much longer to just make it fresh."

"Pipe down," said the microwave. "You're not the only one who can cook," it said.

"I have to agree with the stove," said the wallet. "Bacon is bad enough...but microwave bacon? Not very healthy, Albert."

"Microwave is fine," said the car keys. "It's just breakfast. Let's get cooking so we can move on with our day."

Albert placed the bacon in the microwave and went back to cooking the eggs. He moved them around a bit and placed a lid over the pan so they would cook on top.

"Beep...bacon is done," announced the microwave.

"We haven't finished the eggs yet," said the stove.

"It will give the bacon a chance to cool off," the reading glasses pointed out.

Albert nodded. He got out a plate and gathered up the components of his breakfast. After turning off the stove he set everything down on the table and sat down to eat.

"You have a few emails," reported the cell phone.

Albert adjusted his reading glasses and looked through the messages as he ate his breakfast. "I don't see anything important here," he said. "I didn't ask any of these people to contact me."

"They're all selling things we don't want or need," said the wallet.

"There's one from your editor," said the phone.

"We should definitely take a look at that," said the reading glasses.

Albert looked again and located the email from his editor. "It looks like a new assignment," said Albert after reading it.

"Any travel involved?" asked the car keys.

"No," replied Albert. "I don't have to travel for work," he said with a touch of pride.

"It sounds like our day has gotten a bit busier," said the wallet. "Better finish up and get at those errands."

"I suppose we should," said Albert. He rinsed his plate and set it in the drying rack. Albert gathered up his things and went about the day.

2

Albert was comparing two variations of his favorite toothpaste when he heard a voice to the right call out to him. "Hey…you there." Albert looked over and saw an electric toothbrush sitting in a display holder on the shelf.

"Do you know which of these toothpastes is better?" Albert asked the electric toothbrush. "This one is tartar control but this one strengthens enamel. I want to remove tarter but if I had stronger enamel I might not get the tartar in the first place."

"Why are you asking me?" asked the electric toothbrush.

"You're a toothbrush," said Albert. "I just thought you'd know."

"Listen, I don't know about all that," it replied, "but if you want to get your teeth really clean you should be using an electric toothbrush."

"Thank you," said Albert, "but I prefer a manual toothbrush."

"Manual," replied the electric toothbrush. "Do you drive around in a pedal car?"

"No," said Albert. "I have a regular car."

"No pedals," said the electric toothbrush, "but you're still using a manual toothbrush?"

"I ride a bike sometimes," said Albert. "That has pedals."

"You can go faster in a car than a bike, right?" asked the electric toothbrush.

"Yes," said Albert. "I'm happy with the manual, though. I use this one here as a matter of fact." Albert took his brand of toothbrush off the rack and showed it to the electric toothbrush.

"That model," replied the electric toothbrush. "Buddy, you're lucky your teeth haven't fallen out by now."

"What's wrong with this one?" asked Albert. He pointed to the label. "Look, six out of seven dentists recommend this one."

"That's because the seventh one recommends me," said the electric toothbrush. "Those other six guys, they're just mad because I'm taking away all their business."

Albert walked over to take a closer look at the electric toothbrush. "Is an electric toothbrush faster?" he asked.

"Faster...better...cleaner...whatever you want," said the electric toothbrush. "And I'm on sale this week."

"I don't really need a new toothbrush," said Albert.

"I don't really need to sit on this shelf anymore," said the electric toothbrush.

"I'm sorry," said Albert. "Not today."

"You think about it then," said the electric toothbrush. "When you're scrubbing those bent bristles back and forth across your teeth, just think about my sonic action."

"Sonic action?" asked Albert.

"You heard me," replied the electric toothbrush.

"What does that mean?" Asked Albert.

"It's sonic," said the electric toothbrush.

"But what does that mean?" Asked Albert again.

"Sonic action," repeated the electric toothbrush. "Just think about it."

"I…I will," said Albert.

"Sonic," repeated the electric toothbrush.

"Uh huh," said Albert. He grabbed both types of toothpaste and hastily left the store aisle.

Albert decided he really needed some shirts anyway. He began to look through the racks in the men's department. He found one he thought he might like.

"Albert, don't you think that shirt is a bit extravagant?" asked the wallet as Albert held the shirt up to his chest.

"I don't think so," replied Albert.

"There's a whole rack of reasonable ones over there," pointed out the wallet.

"I don't like those," said Albert.

"Why not?" asked the wallet.

"I don't know…they're not the right blend," Albert replied. "This one is fifty percent cotton."

"Those are one hundred percent cotton," said the wallet.

"I like these patterns better," said Albert.

"Those patterns are obnoxious. You only want it because you saw that actor wearing it on television," explained the wallet.

"So what if I do?" Asked Albert.

"It's not practical," replied the wallet.

"You're the one carrying around all those high interest credit cards," said Albert. "What would you know about practical?"

Albert put his wallet back in his pocket. He walked over to the rack of more reasonably priced shirts and selected a blue one in his size.

Albert walked out of the store. Almost immediately a metal scoop from the nearby ice cream shop began to call to him. "We have caramel swirl," it said. "That's your favorite."

"I could get just a scoop," said Albert.

"Then you won't fit into that shirt," the wallet called out in a muffled voice from Albert's pocket.

"Let me take a look," said the reading glasses from his top pocket. Albert took the reading glasses out of his pocket and put them on. "Ice cream always makes you happy," they said.

"Ice cream does make me happy," concluded Albert. He walked over and purchased a double-scoop of caramel swirl in a waffle cone.

"Thank you for your business," the scoop called as he walked away. Albert wandered the rest of the shopping center while eating the ice cream. Other things called to him along the way, hawking everything from cell phone cases decked out in fake jewels to finely trimmed bonsai plants. Of course, the Zen philosophy of the plants compelled them to admit they would most likely die after a few weeks when Albert would be unable to take care of them.

"Hey fatty, you done eating that yet?" the wallet called from his pocket.

"Maybe I should get one of those new wallet's that holds your money and your phone," Albert replied.

"Oh sure, just toss me aside. Never mind that I've been with you since college. Have you forgotten about Columbia House? I can give those guys your current address in a heartbeat."

"I don't think they're in business anymore," said Albert. "I'm finished, though. We might as well go home."

"Good," said the wallet. "The cell phone cases were getting on my nerves."

3

"Good morning Albert," said the stove cheerily as Albert entered the kitchen. "Shall we cook up some eggs today?" it asked.

"Not today," Albert replied. "I just had eggs the other day."

"It's been almost a week since you had eggs," the stove corrected him.

"I'm going to have cereal,' said Albert. "I could use the iron and the calcium." In truth Albert just didn't feel like cooking that morning. He was anxious to eat and get on with his day.

"Very well then," said the stove. "Enjoy your cold cereal."

"I heard that," said the milk as Albert was taking it out of the fridge. He went to the pantry and looked over his selection of cereal.

"Have some of this," suggested the fruit flavored brand. "I'll make you feel like a kid again…and there's a surprise at the bottom of my box." Albert briefly considered this. Then he realized he'd only eaten that cereal a couple of times since he bought it so it was unlikely he would get to the prize today.

"I'll keep you regular," announced the bran flakes in a low monotone.

"And taste like cardboard," added the corn flakes.

"You think you're that much better?" asked a box of granola-based cereal. "Who gets up in the morning and says 'hey, I'd really like to eat some corn this morning.'"

"Don't listen to any of them Albert," said a box from another shelf on the pantry. "What you need is a nice hot bowl of oatmeal." Albert considered this for a moment. "I have cinnamon flavor," added the box of oatmeal.

"Albert doesn't want mush for breakfast," announced the fruity cereal. "Have a bowl of fun….do you remember the jingle?"

"No….no…." stammered Albert. "Not the jingle. It'll be stuck in my head for hours."

"Fruity bits, those fruity bits," the box began to sing. "Everyone sits for fruity bits…"

"Please no more," Albert implored. "It's already getting in my head."

"But there's three more verses," said the fruity cereal.

Albert quickly shut the pantry door. "Maybe I will have some eggs," he said.

"Good to see you've come to your senses," said the stove.

Albert gathered the milk and eggs and went over to the stove. As he started cooking the eggs he began to sing, "Fruity bits, those fruity bits…."

After breakfast, Albert went into his home office and sat down at the desk. He placed his phone next to the blotter and opened the calculator app on it.

"Bills again?" asked the phone.

"It is the third Thursday," said Albert.

"True," replied the phone.

Albert began to page through his bills and fill out checks for the appropriate number. He used the calculator on the phone to subtract the amount of each check from the current balance. He then carefully wrote the numbers on a log sheet in the check binder.

After about five checks, Albert discovered he had reached the last check of the current book. "There is another book in the bottom left drawer," suggested the reading glasses.

"I know," replied Albert, reaching down to retrieve the fresh book of checks.

"Did you know you can pay all those bills over the computer or even through me?" asked the phone. "Even schedule them to be paid every month."

"Yes, I know," replied Albert.

"Then why don't you?" asked the phone.

"I like this way better," said Albert.

"But isn't it annoying to go through all those pay slips and write out all of those checks?" suggested the phone.

"Nope," said Albert.

"Don't you trust me?"

"Of course I trust you," replied Albert.

"Then how come you never call anyone?" asked the phone.

"That's not true," protested Albert. "I call people all the time. I made a call not twenty minutes ago."

"That call was to your doctor," replied the phone.

"I've known the doctor for twenty years," replied Albert. "I like talking to him."

"You hate the doctor," said the phone.

"I don't mind paying bills this way," said Albert, trying to change the subject.

"But why?" asked the phone.

"What else would we do on the third Thursday?" replied Albert. He placed the fresh book of checks on the desk and continued to work his way through the rest of the stack of bills.

"Let's call your brother," suggested the phone. "You haven't called him in weeks."

"He's very busy," replied Albert.

"Not too busy to talk," said the phone.

"You made a mistake," said the reading glasses. "That should be a six, not a nine."

"That's right," said Albert. "Thank you."

"You're very welcome," said the glasses.

4

Albert stared at the line of traffic before him. He could vaguely make out the flashing lights of emergency vehicles somewhere ahead. He shifted in his seat and adjusted the temperature controls.

"It looks like we may be here awhile," said the car keys.

"I can see that," replied Albert.

"Don't get annoyed with me," protested the keys. "I didn't cause the accident. Why don't you listen to some music?"

"No thanks. I like the quiet," he replied. People in the other cars began to honk their horns. "Maybe I will listen to some music," said Albert. But he didn't turn on the radio.

"What do they think they'll accomplish with that racket?" asked the keys. "Maybe we should honk back."

Albert looked towards the noise. A small blue car was trying to push its way into another lane. Albert didn't understand this. Neither lane appeared to be moving at the moment.

"Perhaps he needs to turn off," suggested his keys. "We're turning off soon, maybe we should follow him."

"I don't know," said Albert.

"Would you let him in?" asked the keys.

Albert thought for a moment. He wasn't sure whether or not he would let the other car move in front of him. He looked at his own position in the traffic jam and realized he was only inches from the car in front of him.

Albert resolved to allow more distance, but was unable to change the situation as long as the traffic did not move.

Albert's pocket began to vibrate. The phone called out "Albert!" "You have a call, Albert," said the phone.

"I'm driving," replied Albert.

Vibration. "Not really," said the phone.

"Yes, I am," said Albert.

Vibration. "You're not actually moving," said the phone.

"That's not the point," said Albert.

Vibration. "I bet it's your brother," said the phone.

"It doesn't matter," said Albert.

Vibration. "Traffic is stopped," said the phone.

"It could move at any moment," said Albert.

Vibration…the vibration stopped midway through. "It looks like you missed the call," said the phone.

Albert looked ahead, back to where the little blue car had given up its attempt to move over.

"He's given up," said the keys.

"I can see that," said Albert.

"So maybe this is our chance to try and get over," said the keys.

"I don't think so," Albert replied.

"You never answered my question," said the keys.

"I don't want to answer," said Albert.

"That's enough of an answer," said the keys.

"I know," said Albert. The traffic continued to inch along until he reached the accident itself. By the time he finally made it back to the house the light was already beginning to fade and he still had to mow the lawn.

The only household chore Albert didn't like was mowing the lawn. In fact, he dreaded doing it each week and looked forward to the fall when the grass would just stop growing. Albert considered the lawn mower to be quite obstinate. It never wanted to start on the first try, it was difficult to turn and always seemed to be pulling away from him.

It had rained frequently over the last month and that meant Albert had to mow the lawn even more often than usual. Reluctantly he went into the garage to fetch the mower. He wheeled it out of the garage and immediately into the back yard.

Albert always started with the backyard. In the back his neighbors couldn't see him struggling to get the lawn mower started. Whenever anything outdoors didn't go well – either the lawn mower, an electric saw or the sprinklers – one of the neighbors always had "suggestions" for Albert.

They always seemed to know everything he was specifically doing wrong and the proper solutions. Except that none of their solutions ever seemed to work either. That usually prompted even more solutions from whichever neighbor happened to be out that particular day.

Once in the backyard, Albert went through the steps to start the lawn mower. As always he had no success on the first try. Nor did the lawn mower start on the second or third try. "Maybe I should just get a new one," said Albert.

He took a deep breath and tried one last time. The lawn mower started right up. "Hello Albert," it said as it roared into life. "You should start with the front yard. It's taller because it gets more sun and it's the area people see the most."

Albert ignored the suggestion and began pushing the lawn mower around the backyard.

"You're chewing up the edges of the beds," scolded the lawn mower. Albert shifted the mower away from the edging. "Now you've left a gap," said the mower.

"I'll double back," said Albert.

"Then you won't get even rows," explained the mower.

Albert felt it pulling away from him and started to hold it back.

"You're going to be at this all day," said the mower.

Albert frowned and maneuvered the law mower around a turn as he reached the fence.

"You need to turn tighter," instructed the mower. "You're going to leave a gap between the rows."

Albert shifted the mower closer to the previous row.

"This row is uneven," said the mower. "Look behind you."

Albert looked behind him to see that his rows did weave a bit. "It's not a baseball field," he grumbled.

"No it's not," said the lawn mower.

5

Albert cleaned the house once every five days…whether or not the rooms were dirty. The bathroom always seemed to need cleaning, if only to remove the hardened bits of soap on the sink and bits of lint on the floor.

The other rooms of the house usually just needed some dusting and a little vacuuming. Albert went over every surface and each floor regardless. He always enjoyed trying out the new cleaning solutions such as special wipes and electronic cleaning devices.

Albert had a collection of disinfecting agents, organic cleaners, magic sponges and even two brands of high-end vacuum. He reasoned this by keeping one of the vacuums upstairs and the other downstairs. Albert had wipes and air freshener cans in just about every room. Although he only cleaned every five days he used the air fresheners several times a day.

"Why do you keep spraying those things? I don't smell anything," said the vacuum. At first Albert had trouble understanding it over the noise of its own motor. "I said, I don't smell anything," repeated the vacuum.

"You don't think it's a bit musty?" Albert asked, realizing what the vacuum had said.

"Not really," Albert replied.

"I do," replied Albert. He had always been overly sensitive towards smells, especially undesirable smells. He attributed it to his years of allergies and sinus trouble.

"I guess it could be fresher in here," the vacuum conceded. "Why don't we just open a window?"

"There was a skunk outside last night," Albert replied. "The smell might still be in the air."

"You should start covering the garbage cans," suggested the vacuum.

"I do," said Albert. "My neighbor doesn't."

"The same one with the car alarm?" asked the vacuum.

"Yes," replied Albert. He picked up the can and sprayed the air freshener again. "That's better," he said.

"I guess so," said the vacuum. "I think we're done with this room. Why don't we move on to the next one?"

"Just a minute," said Albert. He took his reading glasses out of his pocket and placed them on his nose.

"We missed a spot over there," said the glasses.

"How would you know?" asked the vacuum. "Aren't you supposed to be for reading?"

"I was just thinking we'd go over the spot again, just in case," explained the glasses.

"That sounds like a good idea," said Albert.

"But there isn't any paper or anything there," protested the vacuum. No one's even been there since we vacuumed a few days ago."

"How would you know?" asked Albert. "You've been in the closet."

"Oh, I know," said the vacuum. "I just know."

"How about just one time over that spot?" asked the glasses. "It can't hurt and you'll get to spend a few more minutes out of the closet."

"I supposed I can't argue with that," said the vacuum.

"That sounds like a good compromise," said Albert.

"It sounds like a waste of electricity," came the voice of Albert's wallet. It was sitting nearby on the nightstand.

Albert's glasses let out a sigh. "Isn't it always better to double check?"

"That is true," replied the wallet. "I guess I'm onboard."

"It's settled then," said Albert. He steered the vacuum back over to the spot.

"What were we doing again?" asked the vacuum.

6

Albert looked in the mirror and ran a hand over his cheeks and chin. There didn't seem to be much stubble so he considered just using the electric razor. He picked it up.

"Good choice Albert," said the electric razor. "You'll be done quickly with no need for cream or lotion."

"Wait Albert," protested the straight razor from its holder near the sink. "You'll get a cleaner shave with me."

"That's true," said Albert. "But I wasn't planning on going anywhere today."

"What does that matter?" asked the straight razor. "You should still be clean shaven."

"He'll be clean shaven," said the electric razor. "That's my job...and I'm quicker."

Albert knew this was true. He was already getting a late start to the day and he wanted to get on with his tasks.

"Honestly Albert," said the straight razor, "You might as well stop using soap in the shower. Male grooming is extremely important."

"Do you want to get on with your day or not?" Asked the electric razor. "I'll have you ship shape in under five minutes."

Albert agreed. He didn't feel like shaving by hand today. He would do that tomorrow before meeting his editor. Albert turned on the electric razor and pressed it on one of his cheeks. He made only two passes before the electric razor went silent.

Albert held the razor up in front of him and switched the button on and off several times. The razor remained silent. He opened up the bathroom cabinet and took out the chord. Albert plugged in the chord and switched on the button again.

The razor still did not work, so Albert took off the head and shook the razor over the sink. A small amount of hair came out. He put the head back on and tried the button again. The razor continued to be silent.

"Is everything okay?" Asked the straight razor.

Albert looked at the electric razor. It had been a gift from his brother several years before. Albert arrived at lunch with several small cuts on his face. The next time they met his brother gave him the electric razor.

Albert sighed and used the straight razor, nicking himself several times. He dabbed at his face with tissues until the bleeding stopped, then headed downstairs.

There was a knock at the door. The postman greeted him on the doorstep. "Hello Albert," he said cheerily.

Albert nodded back. The postman handed him a package. "I just need you to sign here," he added, giving Albert a slip. Albert signed for the package and took it back inside.

He walked to the office and set it down on the desk. "Something new?" asked the reading glasses.

"Yes," said Albert.

"What is it?" asked the reading glasses.

"Well see in a minute," replied Albert.

He opened the package and removed the item inside. He set it on the desk and smiled. The object was quiet for several minutes.

"It doesn't seem to have anything to say," pointed out the reading glasses.

"Be patient," replied Albert.

"I can make between one and twelve cups of coffee," the new item said at last. Albert wrote this down in his notebook.

The item was quiet once again. "We don't have all day," said the car keys from where they sat on the desk.

"Actually, we do," said Albert. "This assignment is not due for three weeks."

"I have a programmable timer," the item continued. "Many of my parts are machine washable." Albert continued to take notes.

"You can vary the strength of the brew based on the type and amount of coffee you place inside the drip basin." Albert nodded and continued to write.

"Well this is riveting," said the car keys with a sigh. "I suppose you're contractually obligated to listen to this."

"That's not very friendly," said Albert. "And yes, I am contractually obligated to listen to this.

"I come with a lifetime guarantee," said the coffee maker. Albert detected the slightest bit of indignation in its voice. He wrote the declaration down on his notepad.

"I can keep the coffee warm in my shatter-resistant pot for up to three hours after brewing," the coffee maker continued.

"I know I impressed," said car keys sarcastically.

Albert placed the car keys in the top drawer of his desk. They protested in a muffled voice as he closed the drawer.

"To program my timer, begin by holding down the CLOCK button for three seconds to set the hour," continued the coffee maker. Albert struggled a bit to see the button.

"The CLOCK button is above the green indicator light," offered the coffee maker.

Albert moved further forward, then leaned back to try and see the button. "I'll have to get my reading glasses out," he said. They were in the drawer with the car keys.

"I understand," said the coffee maker.

Albert retrieved the reading glasses from the drawer and put them on his face. "...and you could use an oil change." Apparently, the car keys had not stopped ranting in the drawer.

"Are you finished?" asked the coffee maker.

"Are you?" asked the car keys.

"My clock isn't even set yet," said the coffee maker.

"I couldn't see the button," explained Albert. He went about setting the clock on the coffee maker and the car keys remained silent from that point.

The coffee maker continued to speak for two hours. Albert was careful to write everything down. He also drank several cups of coffee.

"That's going to keep you up all night," said the car keys. Albert was sure he detected a note of triumph.

"You're probably right," replied Albert. "I think I'll go for a walk in the woods and collect my thoughts."

"Well at least that means we'll be getting out of the house," replied the car keys.

7

Albert liked to walk in the woods near his home. The woods were the one place in Albert's life that was always a little different. He liked to imagine the trees and bushes shifting themselves around when he wasn't there, perhaps even occasionally dropping a few twigs or half-rotted log into place.

Nothing in the forest ever spoke to Albert. He assumed this was because everything was simply too busy with its own work. Albert was careful to empty his pockets at the car before starting on the path. He brought the cell phone for safety but always turned it off.

Albert always strolled the well worn path a total of three times. The first time through he concentrated on the scenery to his right. The second time through he concentrated on the scenery to his left. The third time through he concentrated on the scenery below him.

He was careful not to trip or run into a tree while looking down. After many afternoons of practice, he had gotten used to casting his eyes at a downward angle while still training his peripheral vision on the objects on either side of him.

He also did not stroll while looking upward. On one occasion he had tried walking a fourth time along the path while concentrating up, but this had led to a twisted ankle and a large cut on his forearm.

Albert enjoyed the third stroll most of all. Details and activities along the forest floor fascinated him. He liked to watch the hustle and bustle along its edges. To Albert it seemed like an everlasting construction site.

Workers of all types were always wandering here and there, going about their area of expertise.

The beetles were the excavators, pushing and moving the sand. The caterpillars were the garbage disposers, munching away leaves and other bits of debris. The bees acted like foreman, wearing their special black and yellow uniforms and buzzing about the site. They appeared to watch over the other workers.

In Albert's mind the ants were the common laborers of the site. Ants were always busy moving items here or there, or just hurrying along to someplace or something that needed their attention.

Albert tried to follow them a couple of times but couldn't keep up. He would lose them in the brush or tall bits of grass. Occasionally, one of the ants would be carrying a leaf or stick or some other bit of food, not unlike a worker might carry around a wooden beam or bucket of nails.

If Albert was an insect, he was sure he'd be an ant - always busy and always in the background. Albert likened himself to one of the workers carrying a bit of leaf or crust of bread. The single morsel above his head didn't amount to much by itself, but it was part of a larger whole.

Albert liked to believe he was always part of something larger, even though he couldn't see very far down the path in front of him. Watching the ants almost convinced him it didn't matter if he wasn't able to see that far down the path. It certainly didn't matter to the ants.

Albert was watching the ants when he heard something. It was a light, creaky voice that struggled to speak. Albert could tell it had not spoken in some time.

He scanned back along the path until he could determine the source.

The voice was coming from a small black case partially buried under a pile of fallen leaves. Albert moved the debris aside and picked up the case. He brushed away the dust and opened it. Inside he found a watch. Albert recognized the style as what used to be known as a barrel or tank because of the elongated shape.

"My father used to wear one of these," said Albert. He took a few moments to listen but heard nothing further from the watch.

"Maybe it just needs bit of oil," said Albert. He put the watch in his pocket and continued his walk.

8

The car alarm had been going off for about fifteen minutes when the clock finally said something to Albert. "Aren't you going to do anything about that?"

"What do you want me to do? It's not my car," said Albert.

"It belongs to the guy who lives next door," said the clock. 'You know that. It's the third time it's gone off this week."

"I think he's a sound sleeper," Albert explained.

"Well go over and wake him up," suggested the clock.

"I don't want to be one of those guys," Albert replied.

"What guys?" asked the clock. "You mean those guys who get a good night's sleep?"

"You know…one of those guys who goes over and knocks on doors," said Albert. "The same guys who shush you during the movie."

"That's right," said the clock. "Those are the guys who get a good night's sleep."

"That's right, Albert," called his reading glasses from the end table. "You don't want any trouble. It'll stop soon enough."

"You could call him," suggested the cell phone from its charger across the room.

"I don't want to be one of those guys, either," replied Albert.

"Those guys get a full night's sleep too," said the clock.

"What do you care anyway?" said Albert. "You're just the clock."

"I get up the same time as you. A few seconds before to be exact."

Albert sighed. He rolled over and placed the pillow over his head. He cared more about not hearing the clock any more than not hearing the car alarm. Albert had never much cared for the clock. It was obnoxious… whether or not it was in the process of waking him up.

Sometimes Albert even considered that the clock purposely didn't go off when he needed it most - like the day he had the doctor's appointment. The alarm never went off and he missed the appointment. He was unable to get an appointment for another three weeks.

Just then the car alarm stopped. Albert rolled back over and looked out his window. Another one of his neighbors was walking away from the car holding a pair of scissors. The owner of the car didn't come out and didn't seem to notice. Albert leaned back against the headboard.

"Finally," said the clock. Its face was digital but Albert was sure he could detect a smug look on it. He reached over and smacked down the snooze button. In the distance, a different car alarm went off.

9

Albert parked his car and made his way down the street to the restaurant where he always met his brother. Along the way he passed a jewelry store and stopped to look in the front window.

He could hardly believe his eyes. The third watch from the left was an exact match to the watch he'd found on the trail the other day.

"I see that you have fine taste sir," said the watch. "In addition to classic styling that goes with everything from business casual to formal wear, my Swiss engineered mechanism keeps perfect time. A matching winder is also available."

Albert took the old watch out of his pocket and held it up to the glass.

"Oh dear," said the new watch. "That piece has been very mistreated."

"I found it along a trail," said Albert.

"Such a pity," said the new watch. "Although the newer models, such as myself, are much more reliable."

"I'm thinking of having it fixed," said Albert.

"Actually," replied the new watch, "that model loses as much as one second per week."

Albert looked at the old watch. "Maybe it can be adjusted," he said.

"No," explained the new watch, "it's attributed to the old tooling and the individual construction of each unit. Once the old shop was bought out by the multinational brand, that substandard method was replaced by a modern production line."

"Are you saying this watch was made by one person?" asked Albert.

"Exactly," replied the new watch.

"And you're made by many people," said Albert.

"Several machines actually," said the new watch.

"Oh," said Albert.

"But people observe the machines…I think," added the new watch.

"And I suppose there are hundreds of watches like you," said Albert.

"Thousands," corrected the new watch. It was quiet for a moment. "What do you want with that old watch anyway?" it asked almost defensively.

"I'd like to find this watch's owner," said Albert.

"Looks to me like it would be better without that person," said the new watch.

"They may have lost it by accident," said Albert. "Do you think this store would know who bought this watch?" asked Albert.

"I doubt it," said the new watch. "This store has only carried my brand of watch for three years."

"I see," said Albert. "Well thank you anyway."

"You're welcome…I think," said the new watch. "If you ever need more accurate time…"

"I think this watch will do fine," said Albert, walking away from the jewelry store.

Albert entered the restaurant to find his brother already seated at the table. He gave a quick wave and Albert joined him at the table.

"How are you, Albert?"

"I'm fine, James," said Albert. "How are you?"

"I'm doing well," his brother replied. "I just got a promotion at work and Jane's been voted onto the local school board."

"That sounds important," said Albert.

"It is," replied his brother. "So, are you keeping busy?"

"Busy? Yes. I guess so." Albert wasn't exactly sure what would constitute "busy" as his brother saw it.

"Do you know what you need, Albert? You need a hobby," said his brother.

"Don't you just hate people who answer their own questions?" commented a voice to Albert's right. He looked in that direction, where a reproduction of Edvard Munch's the Scream was crammed onto the wall with several other reproductions such as Starry Night and a couple of Monets.

"And what is this blowhard talking about with this hobby stuff anyway?" continued the painting. "If I wasn't already screaming…"

Albert smiled at the painting.

"Albert? Are you okay?" asked his brother.

"Huh? Yes, I'm fine. I'm sorry," replied Albert. "I was just distracted.

"How are you doing?" asked his brother. Albert saw that he was rubbing at the scar tissue on his cheek.

"Does it hurt?" Albert asked, gesturing at his brother's cheek.

His brother immediately withdrew his hand from his face. "No," he replied. "It just gets dry."

"When it gets sunny out," said Albert.

"I have to keep it covered from the sun, Albert," replied his brother. "It's a sunburn scar."

"Oh," said Albert. "I'm sorry…"

"Let's not talk about that," his brother cut him off.

Albert started to speak but his brother shook his head. "How is your job going?" he asked changing the subject.

"It's fine," Albert replied. "I just finished the manual for a new model of coffee maker."

"Don't you ever aspire to do anything different?" asked his brother.

"I like what I do," replied Albert.

"And you're very good at it," added the painting with confidence.

"And I'm sure you're very good at it," said his brother. His tone was noticeably different than the painting.

"Yes, I am very good at it," confirmed Albert.

"I'm sure you are," said his brother. "But don't you want to do something more important?"

"What I do is important," Albert protested.

"Judging by the amount of coffee people guzzle down in this restaurant, I have to agree," said the painting.

"I can still get you an interview where I work," said his brother. "You'd get out more…be around people. It would be good for you."

"I don't think so," said Albert.

His brother signaled the waiter over. "I have to get back," he said. "You should come to the house to see Jane and the girls."

"Won't that be a treat?" said the painting. It was the Scream's turn for sarcasm. "Then he and his wife can patronize you at the same time." This made Albert laugh out loud.

"I'm sorry," he said. Across from him, James just shook his head.

10

"Good evening, Albert," said the microwave. "What are we having tonight?"

Albert greeted the microwave with a smile. For some reason it was always cheery, perhaps because it was the appliance he used the most. "Just some soup," he replied.

"Excellent choice. May I suggest you compliment it with some of that fresh Romano cheese in the fridge and some water crackers?"

"I'm sold," said Albert. After starting the soup in the microwave, he went to the refrigerator and took out the cheese. He cut several slices and placed them on a small plate.

Albert added several crackers to the plate and placed it on the kitchen table. By this time the soup was finished and he removed it from the microwave and set it next to the cheese and cracker plate.

"You can heat up soup on the burner," protested the stove.

"It's not as fast," said Albert turning on the small television in the kitchen.

"Cooking should be part of the experience of eating," replied the stove. "You used to make your own soup. I once heard you say you'd never eat soup from a can."

"I guess I'm expanding my horizons," Albert said. He sat down and began to eat, flipping through the channels.

"You realize this is only one step away from eating straight from the can," complained the stove. "Next thing you know you'll be eating over the sink."

"Then he couldn't see the television," said the microwave.

"Television during dinner," said the stove. "How uncivilized."

"See if there's a cooking show on," suggested the microwave.

"That sounds good," confirmed Albert. He went through the channels that usually had cooking shows on but couldn't find anything at the moment. He finally settled on an infomercial about a food dehydrator.

About half way through Albert realized he'd written the manual for the device two years ago. He ended up making some notes to send the manufacturer about mistakes in the commercial.

"This is what comes from not cooking your food on the stove or in the oven like a civilized person," lamented the stove.

"In this case I have to agree," said the microwave. "There must be something better on than this."

Albert resumed flipping through the channels until he discovered a program talking about national parks. "It would be nice to visit these places one day," said Albert.

"Then why don't you go," said the keys.

"I think I'll finish my soup," said Albert.

"This is excellent work Albert," said his editor. "As always, of course," he added.

"Thank you," replied Albert. The two had been going over the manual for the coffeemaker. "It really does make good coffee."

"What's that now?" asked the editor. He was leafing through the pages.

"I said it makes good coffee," repeated Albert.

"What does?" asked the editor.

"The coffeemaker," explained Albert.

"What coffeemaker?" asked the editor. "Oh, you mean this one. Of course." He folded closed the manuscript. "I know I already said it, but great work Albert. Almost makes me want to buy one of these."

"You don't have a coffeemaker?" asked Albert.

His editor looked at him for a moment. "Of course not," he replied at last. "That's why they have coffee shops. Why would I make my own?"

Albert looked puzzled. "No one makes their own coffee anymore," explained the wallet from Albert's pocket. "It's why no one has any money."

"Albert?" asked the editor.

"Huh?" said Albert, looking up.

"I think I lost you there for a moment," said the editor. "Anyway I think I may have a much bigger assignment for you next time."

"Oh?" asked Albert.

"Definitely," said the editor. "It even involves some travel."

"Oh, I don't think…" started Albert.

"You are my 'go to' guy," said the editor. "You're going to love this next assignment. I've got at least three writers who want to work on it but you've earned it."

"But…" Albert stammered.

"You'll also have a chance to be creative," said his editor. "I know you've got it in you."

"I don't know," said Albert. "My degree is in journalism. I've only written non-fiction."

"This isn't exactly fiction," replied the editor. "Just a chance to be a bit more inventive. But I'm getting a bit ahead of things. I have to nail the contract down first."

"You do that," said the keys.

"I'd really like to know more about this," said the wallet. Albert nodded in agreement with the wallet.

"Glad to see you're onboard," said the editor after seeing the nod.

"I think…" began Albert.

"More details later," said the editor. He looked at his watch. "Anyway…have to run Albert." The editor left before Albert could say another word.

"Intriguing," said the keys from their spot on the hanger nearby.

"I like where this is going," said the cell phone.

"Don't you start," said the wallet. "I don't like the sound of this at all. Not one bit."

"We need to learn more about this," said the reading glasses. "Let's call him up later and see if he'll tell us more."

"Good idea," said the wallet. "We need to get all the details about this. We don't want to rush into anything."

Albert just stood in the doorway and watched the editor get in his car and leave. He wasn't sure what to make of things.

Albert went back inside. He tried to work on some household items but was too distracted by the editor's news. It was too early to start dinner so he decided to watch some television. Albert turned on the TV and clicked the Guide button on the remote to review the available programs.

"Witness the greatest battle in history!" Shouted one of the stations. "Six monster trucks enter but only one will leave."

"Learn the secrets of classic French sauces," announced another. "Today on the Grappling Gourmet we'll start part one of our journey – butter and flour."

"There's nothing on television," said the wallet. "As usual. You could probably cut the cable bill by half, Albert."

"He's barely started to look," said the car keys. "The monster truck program sounded pretty good."

"Find a good drama," said the cell phone. "Something where people have to face their differences and work together."

"That's exactly what's happening on the truck rally," said the car keys.

"I don't know if facing their differences by running into each other qualifies," said the reading glasses.

"Yes," agreed Albert. He continued to look through the channel guide.

"It was the greatest influence on modern civilization," began the next channel. Albert was somewhat intrigued. "And it wiped out half the population. Today on Medieval Times…"

Albert flipped to the next section of the guide. "I don't think so," said Albert.

"That one actually sounded good," said the wallet.

"There's no accounting for taste," said the cell phone.

"It was the story of a man and a woman," explained another station. "…and a dog…."

"This one sounds good," said the cell phone.

"….and a cat….and a bird named Rupert," it concluded.

"Maybe not," said Albert.

"Today on Too Fast for TV," said the next station, "we'll take this late model sedan apart piece by piece and reassemble it as the quickest golf cart every created."

Albert looked up at the clock and decided it wasn't too early to start dinner after all. He turned off the television and went to the kitchen.

"At least leave the monster truck rally on," said the car keys. Albert just shook his head and went to the refrigerator.

12

"Nothing but bad news today Albert," declared the newspaper. "Fires…murders…war…it's all terrible I'm afraid."

Albert put on his reading glasses and glanced over the front page. "Someone local won the lottery," he said.

"Died of shock the very next day," replied the newspaper. "Apparently he was so excited he had a heart attack. Dropped dead with the ticket still in his hand. Story is continued on page sixteen if you want the details."

"Maybe I'll skip ahead to the weather" said Albert.

"Rain….all rain," said the newspaper.

"Every day?" asked the reading glasses.

"Might was well be," said the newspaper.

"What page has the financials?" asked Albert.

"Stocks are all down," replied the newspaper. "Dow…Nasdaq…everything is in the red."

"Fashion?" suggested the reading glasses.

"Everything new is old, everything old is new," replied the newspaper.

"Maybe just the comics then," said Albert.

"Not funny," said the newspaper. "Comics haven't been funny in ten years. Just a bunch of political commentary and jokes about office cubicles and the Internet."

Albert flipped through the pages of the paper. One page had a story about a three alarm fire. The opposite page described a slew of burglaries in a town nearby. A man got hit by a train. A woman was caught selling counterfeit designer handbags.

"See," said the newspaper, "all bad news. Don't say I didn't warn you."

Albert flipped to the back of the paper and glanced at the comics. A man and a woman were sitting in a meeting. The man at the front was showing them a chart on a screen. The man was saying to the woman, "is that a positive upturn paradigm or a proactively shifting downturn?"

"That is not very funny," said the reading glasses.

"I'm not even sure what that means," said Albert.

Underneath the office comic was a superhero comic. In the first panel the hero was talking to a young woman near a blank parking space. "Are you sure you locked your car?" he asked. "Yes," she replied. The second panel was a close up of the woman's face. Tears rolled down both of her cheeks. "The plans were in there," she was saying. The man and woman were both in the third panel. "Then we'll just have to go after it," said the hero.

"That's it?" Asked Albert. "How long does it take to find out what happens?"

"No one even knows," said the newspaper. "They've been in front of that blank parking space for three weeks now."

Albert kept flipping through the pages of the paper. "This is all bad," he said. "I don't know why I even read the paper."

"No one does," said the newspaper. "Everyone gets their information from somewhere else these days."

Albert just shook his head and set the newspaper aside. He turned his attention to the old watch he'd found in the woods. He picked up a small cloth from the desk and rubbed the face.

"I don't know why you brought that old thing home," huffed the wallet.

"Maybe we should try oiling it," suggested the reading glasses.

"I'm worried that if I open the back we may not get it closed again," said Albert. "Many of these old watches require special tools to open and close."

"That's a prudent course of action," said the wallet. "At least you're being reasonable about that. No sense losing what little worth it has by not working on it properly."

Albert turned the watch over again and stared at the face. The hands almost looked as though they wanted to move and he thought he heard a faint series of clicks coming from the watch.

"That could be the gears trying to move," said Albert, observing the sound.

"Or breaking down for good," said the wallet. "That watch is probably beyond repair."

"It called to me in the woods," said Albert.

"You were probably just hearing someone else on the path," said the wallet.

"Let's just open it and be done with it," came the voice of the keys." At first Albert was startled. He'd forgotten he'd set the keys down on the tray at the edge of the desk.

"I don't know," said Albert.

"Come on, Albert," said the phone from the other side of the desk. "Let's open it up and see what it has to say."

Albert sighed and stared at the watch. He was anxious to hear the stories it might be willing to tell him. "If it breaks…"

"It's already broken," said the reading glasses. "Maybe the others are right. It might help if we opened the watch up and oiled it."

Albert thought for a few minutes. "Okay," he said finally. "I may even have a tool."

"Of course you do," said the wallet. "I should have known."

Albert pulled out a very fine pair of pliers and flipped the watch over. He carefully wedged the pliers into the seam of the watch and began to spread them apart. After a moment the back of the case lifted away from the front.

Albert set the back of the watch down along with a rubber insert designed to keep the inside of the watch dry. He stared at the small cogs, springs and wheels inside.

He set the watch down on the blotter of the desk and opened another drawer. Albert took out a small vial of oil and placed a few drops into the inside of the watch. He then wound the watch a couple of turns.

"Well?" asked the keys.

"It wound a bit easier that time," replied Albert. "But the oil probably needs to soak into the gears."

"That figures," said the keys.

"You need to be patient," said the wallet. For once the reading glasses had to concur, and even if the phone seemed to light up in agreement.

13

Albert walked into the restaurant and tentatively looked around.

"Hello," said the hostess. "Are you ready to be seated or are you waiting for the rest of your party?" she asked.

"I'm by myself," said Albert.

"Says you," said his wallet in a muffled voice from his pocket.

"Hush now," said the phone. "You're being rude as usual."

"That's certainly not a problem," replied the hostess. "Sometimes a quiet lunch is the best."

"Fat chance of that with the cell phone around," said the wallet.

"I'm surprised you even let him come here today," said the phone. "You know this will cost money."

"It certainly wasn't my idea," said the wallet. "Albert just went shopping yesterday. Plenty of food in the fridge."

"Sir?" asked the hostess.

"I'm sorry," said Albert.

"That's okay," said the hostess. "I'll show you to your table." The hostess led him forward. She started towards the far right side.

"Actually," said Albert. "I was wondering if I could have that table there." He gestured towards a table in the middle with a clearer view of the Munch painting. "It's just a two top anyway."

"Absolutely," replied the hostess. "This way please." On the way over to the other table she asked Albert if he had worked in a restaurant since he mentioned an industry term.

"No," replied Albert. "But I did write a manual for restaurant software last year."

"That explains it then," said the hostess. "Enjoy your lunch."

"Thank you," said Albert as he sat down at the table.

Albert watched as the waitress removed the second set of plates and silverware from the table. He was suddenly very self conscious about being in the restaurant by himself. He seemed to be the only one eating alone.

Albert felt a trickle of sweat running down his cheek and was about to get up to leave the restaurant when he heard a friendly voice.

"Hello, Albert," said the painting of the Scream. "It's nice to see you again."

Albert immediately felt a bit calmer. "It's good to see you again, too."

"How is your brother?" asked the painting.

"I have no idea," said Albert. It was true, he hadn't spoken to his brother since they had lunch a week ago.

"How excellent for you, then," said the painting.

"He's a good man," said Albert. "In spite of me." Albert said no more and looked down at the menu.

14

"The time…" said a creaky voice from across the room. Albert looked up from the book he as flipping through and glanced around the room. He was unsure whether or not he'd actually heard anything, so he went back to his book.

"The time is…" said the voice again. It squeaked and cracked its way through a few more words. "The time is three forty…" it said.

Albert decided the voice was coming from the desk. He put the book back on the shelf and walked over to the desk. "Hello?" said Albert tentatively.

Looking down at the desk Albert realized it was coming from the old barrel watch. "Hello…" he said again.

"Three forty…" stammered the watch.

"Do you need some more oil?" asked Albert.

"Three forty.." repeated the watch.

Albert sat down at the desk and took out the small vial of oil. He put a couple of more drops into the watch and wound the dial a few times to move the gears. This time the watch actually began to tick.

"The time is three forty-six," said the watch, speaking much clearer now.

"It must have been a long while since you've had any kind of service," said Albert. "I don't think anyone was following the instructions in your manual."

"The time is three forty-seven," replied the watch.

"Apparently," said Albert. Since the watch was ticking once again, Albert went ahead and used the dials to set it to the correct time. He could see by the clock on the wall it was not three forty-six or forty-seven.

"The time is one twenty-two," said the watch after it had been adjusted.

"Yes," said Albert. "Let's see if I can clean this up a bit," said Albert. He picked up the small cloth and began to wipe the face. After the glass was clear and turned his attention to the back of the watch.

As he continued to wipe he was able to see it had an inscription. Albert put on his reading glasses. It read: "For TM. Much appreciation and good fortune."

"That's interesting," said the glasses. "It looks like this watch was a gift for someone."

"It appears that way," said Albert.

"That looks like it was put on there a long time ago," said the reading glasses.

Albert flipped the watch back over and looked at the face.

"The time is one twenty-three," said the watch.

"That's too bad," said the reading glasses. "It was probably an interesting story."

"It probably was," agreed Albert. He held the bottom of the watch under his desk lamp. "A good story indeed."

15

Albert stared at the three different color receptacles. "This keeps getting more complicated," he said.

"Blue for cardboard, green for plastic and red for glass," said the wallet.

Albert picked up a cardboard box and tossed into into the blue bin. "That was easy enough," he said.

Next came a plastic seltzer bottle. "Green box," said the seltzer bottle. "I'm hoping to come back as something else."

"Like what?" asked Albert.

"A water bottle," said the seltzer.

"That's just seltzer without the bubbles," pointed out the wallet.

Albert pulled out the next item. It was a box from some frozen waffles. "Cardboard," it announced. "I'm coming back as a gift box."

"Trash," said the wallet.

"I beg your pardon," said the waffle box.

"You have a coating," explained the wallet. "It makes you hard to recycle."

"That's just my shine," said the waffle box. "It makes my waffles look hot and crispy."

"Crispy or not," said the wallet. "It makes you hard to recycle."

"Sorry," said Albert. He tossed the waffle box in the trash.

The next item was a pizza box. "I am clearly cardboard," it said.

"Food contamination," said the wallet. "Trash."

Albert opened the pizza box. There was a large grease stain on the underside of the lid and even a few bits of cheese stuck to it. "Sorry," said Albert. He put the pizza box in the trash can.

Albert picked up another cardboard box. He was about to throw it into the blue container when he noticed a stain on it. "I don't even know what that's from," he said.

"It could be food," said the wallet.

"Or maybe it just got wet," said the reading glasses. Albert consider this for a moment and then threw the box into the blue container.

"I hope that wasn't food Albert," said the wallet.

Albert reached down for the next item. It was a plastic orange juice bottle.

"You need to rinse that out," explained the wallet.

Albert sighed and carried the juice bottle over to the sink by the laundry. He rinsed the inside before tossing it into the container for plastics.

"I'm next," said a voice below. Albert reached down and picked up a pile of junk mail. A restaurant coupon was sitting on top. "I'm hoping to come back as something useful," said the coupon.

"You mean like a greeting card or something?" asked Albert.

"I'd settle for coming back as a more useful coupon," it replied.

Albert finished up with the recycling and went back inside the house.

"You seem distracted," said the wallet. "Are you still thinking about the inscription on that watch, Albert?"

"Not really," replied Albert. "Just a passing interest I suppose."

"Passing interest?" continued the wallet. "You printed out a copy and put it on the front of the refrigerator."

"Don't you find it the least bit intriguing?" asked Albert.

"Not in the least," replied the wallet.

"I'm surprised," said the keys from their hook near the pantry. "You usually get lost in the details."

"I don't get lost in the details," said the wallet. "I just understand the importance of being correct."

"For TM. Much appreciation and good fortune," said Albert.

"I remember it from the first time you read it," said the wallet.

"I think it's very interesting," said the cell phone from where it was sitting on the kitchen table. "I'd like to know more about it."

"I agree," said Albert. "I'd like to find out what it means."

"Yes," said the keys. "If we can figure it out then we can move on to something else."

"You are between assignments," said the phone. "You have some free time."

"Albert was going to use this time to go over next year's budget numbers," said the wallet.

"Next year's budget?" said the keys. "We're not even that far into this year. I vote for finding out more about the inscription."

"Albert, how would you even go about finding anything out about that watch?" said the wallet.

Albert thought for a moment. He looked at the inscription on the fridge again and a thought came to him. "I could speak with a watch repairman. He might at least know a bit more about the watch itself."

"Great idea, Albert," said the phone.

"I think there's even a repairman in town," said Albert. "I had my grandfather's pocket watch repaired there a couple of years ago."

"That sounds like a plan," said the keys. "We can go after lunch. Leave the wallet here to work on the budget."

16

"A beautiful piece," said the repairman holding up the old watch to the light. You said you found it in the woods?"

"That's right," said Albert.

"Don't tell him too much," said the wallet. "He's already sizing you up."

"You don't see many of these anymore," continued the repairman. "The style isn't as popular as it used to be, but it'll always be a classic in my mind."

"It's losing a couple of minutes each day," said Albert.

"I'm not surprised," said the repairman. "It probably hasn't been serviced in a long time. I can give it a once over if you like."

"Here it comes," said the wallet.

"I did put some oil in it," said Albert.

"Yes," said the repairman. "I can see that...it also looks like you separated the case without the proper tools."

Albert was embarrassed and looked down at the counter. The repairman seemed to realize he'd over stepped a bit.

"All and all not a terrible job," said the repairman. "No scratches."

Albert looked back up. "I tried to be careful," he said.

"For these watches it's just safer to use the manufacturer's tools," explained the repairman. "Shouldn't be too hard to fix up. Cost you about forty dollars."

"Forty dollars?" protested the wallet. "I knew that watch would end up costing you money."

"Stop being so cheap," said the phone from the clip on Albert's belt. "Don't you care about the watch being able to do its job again?"

"Makes no difference to me," said the wallet.

"That sounds fine," Albert said the repairman. He took a credit card out of his wallet.

"Ask him about the inscription," reminded the cell phone.

"I almost forgot," said Albert. "Would you happen to know anything about the inscription?"

"Much appreciation and good fortune?" quoted the repairman.

"Yes," said Albert. "Have you seen it before?"

"I haven't," said the repairman. "But this model of watch certainly would have made a fine gift. Major event I would think….anniversary…graduation…that sort of thing."

"He has no idea," said the wallet.

The repairman looked up at the ceiling and scratched his head for a moment. "You know who you should talk to?" he said.

Albert shook his head.

"Jenkinson. He's got a shop about fifty miles from here. He's been in the business for years. In fact he was a dealer for this brand and I believe he did a lot of corporate gifts. I'll write the address down for you."

"Thank you," said Albert.

"Make sure you talk to the old man. He's probably in the back. The son runs the shop now. He knows nothing."

17

"I say you go to visit the other jeweler today," said the car keys.

"He can't go today," said the wallet. "He has too many tasks already. Perhaps next week."

"If you can't go today you should at least call," said the cell phone.

"No time for that either," said the wallet. "Besides, he hasn't even planned a route. And who knows if anyone at the other jewelry store can help."

"The other man seem to think so," said the reading glasses. "It can't hurt try."

"I have a lot to do today," said Albert. "The last product manual needs some changes and I have some shopping and cleaning."

"That's right, Albert," said the wallet. "And you don't know how long it will take to get to the other store."

"It's about an hour away," said the car keys.

"That's not too far," added the cell phone.

"That's not accounting for traffic," said the wallet. "You should research the route more before going there."

"Perhaps next week would be better," said Albert. "I'll have the changes finished by then and the weather is supposed to be good."

"That's right," said the wallet. "Rain most of today. You don't want to drive that far in the rain. Especially for something you don't need."

"I wonder what the watch thinks about all this," said the cell phone.

Albert thought about this for a moment. He took the watch out of the desk drawer and stared at it for a moment. It was quiet except for the ticking movement of its gears.

"Well?" asked the wallet.

"Give it a moment," said the reading glasses.

Albert continued to stare at the watch. "The time is nine forty-three," it said finally.

"Plenty of time to take a trip," said the car keys.

"I agree," said the phone.

"The morning is almost over," objected the wallet. "Albert should have started on those edits a half hour ago."

Albert set the watch down and glanced at the feedback he'd gotten from the manufacturer off the coffeemaker. He had originally hoped to finish all the changes the night before, but he had gotten tired.

"Maybe I'll just make a few more edits," said Albert. "Then I won't feel so bad about leaving." Albert continued to work. He didn't stop until he heard the watch speak again.

"The time is twelve fifty-seven," it announced.

Albert glanced at the watch and then checked the time on the clock on the wall. "It's past lunch," he said. He realized he was hungry and would have to get something to eat. "And I still have errands to run."

"That settles it," said the wallet. "You cannot go to the other jewelry store today."

"I have to agree," said the reading glasses. "Better to finish the items you need to get done."

"Yes," said Albert. "The watch will have to wait for another day." He put the watch back in the drawer where he could no longer hear it tick.

18

Albert was overdue for a walk in the woods. The day was mild enough to have the windows down so he could already smell the plants as he pulled into the parking space. He put the wallet and the reading glasses in the glove compartment. He turned the cell phone off before placing it in his pocket.

Albert got out of the car and hid the keys in a small magnetic case underneath it. It was the only way he could have some peace and quiet.

After double checking to make sure the car was locked, Albert made his way to the start of the path. He glanced at the guidepost and decided to take the meadow path today.

After a short time the trees along the path opened up to a large field. The meadow was filled with high grasses and wildflowers that came up to about Albert's chest. He followed the path as it wound its way to and fro, stopping occasionally to take a closer look at a flower or read a placard with the name of a plant.

While taking a closer look at a particularly vibrant blue flower, the thought occurred to Albert that he should right a book about plants. The more he thought about it the more he liked the idea. Albert never wrote about anything but things. The closest he'd ever gotten to writing about something living was a manual about an indoor herb garden. Even that time his editor demanded he finish the manual before any of the herbs had begun to sprout from the small vials of dirt.

Albert continued to think about the book as he made his way along the path to the other side of the meadow. He pictured himself at the desk, glancing down at notes and sketches of plants, writing about the effects of soil chemistry and rainfall. Albert could picture the chapter headings, see the artwork on the cover.

The title of the book wasn't clear, but he saw his name in large letters across the bottom. The idea of his name in print fascinated him. Albert pictured it in different fonts and colors, centered or perhaps off to the right or left. He imagined his brother, the hostess at the restaurant or the watch repairman picking up the book and seeing his name.

Albert became so lost in these thoughts that he was surprised when he came to the point where the path terminated back at the parking lot. Albert didn't want to stop thinking about the book. Instead of going to the car, he turned around and walked the path again.

19

"You're running late," announced the alarm clock. Albert looked over at the time. He would have to get on the road soon if he wanted to get to the other jewelry store at a decent hour. He quickly slipped on his socks and went to his closet to pick out a pair of shoes.

"Right here Albert," said the sneakers. Albert wore sneakers most of the days he left the house. Around the house he preferred to wear slippers with rubber soles.

"You're going on a trip today," said his dress shoes. "You'll want to look nice."

"He's going to see a jeweler about an old watch," said the sneakers. "I think that's more of a casual occasion."

"Long drive today," announced a pair of canvas shoes in a laid back voice. "Go for comfort, man."

"How about wearing something different?" suggested a pair of boat shoes. Albert had bought the boat shoes on sale a couple of years ago. At the time he liked the color but now he rarely wore them.

"Nonsense," said the dress shoes. "You should look professional. People are always more willing to help someone who looks professional."

"That is a good point," said Albert. He started to reach for the dress shoes.

"You should probably change that shirt as well," said the dress shoes. "And consider adding a tie." Albert stopped and scratched his head.

"Pay no attention to those stuffy old things," said the sneakers. "Go with what you know."

"Go for comfort man," said the canvas shoes.

"This seems like a great opportunity for a change of pace," said the boat shoes.

Albert thought about wearing the boat shoes. He felt bad for them, realizing he'd probably only worn them three or four times. Albert picked them up off the shelf. "Very stiff," he observed.

"We're stiff because you never wear us," said the boat shoes.

Albert could not deny this, however he still didn't want to be that uncomfortable. "I'm sorry," he said and put them back down.

"Just give us to Goodwill and be done with it," muttered the boat shoes.

Albert thought about the long drive he had ahead of him and picked up the canvas shoes. "These would definitely be more comfortable for the trip," he said.

"Now you're talking man," said the canvas shoes. "Be comfortable. Laid back. You probably don't even need to take that drive today. Just slip us on and sit out back. You can go to the jeweler tomorrow."

"Time is wasting Albert," said the alarm clock. Albert nodded and picked up the sneakers.

"How predictable," said the other pairs of shoes.

"Yes I am," said Albert with a smile. He wiggled his toes around in the sneakers. They felt just fine to him.

"You're really doing this?" asked the wallet as Albert came downstairs. "You're driving an hour to talk to an old man about a watch you found in the woods."

"Just think of it as an adventure," said the car keys.

Albert nodded. 'That's right, an adventure," he said.

"Who are you trying to convince?" asked the wallet. "Me or you?"

Albert said nothing further but continued to drive until he reached the small town containing the jewelry store. The store was the only occupied storefront along the crumbling downtown street.

Albert parked in front of the store and went inside. A young man was reading a magazine behind the counter. He did not look up when Albert entered.

"Hello?" Albert asked tentatively.

"Can I help you?" asked the young man without looking up from his magazine.

"I'm looking for someone who can help me with a watch," said Albert.

"Just tell me which one you want and I'll get it out of the case," replied the man. He still did not look up from the magazine.

"It's about an old watch," said Albert taking the barrel watch out of his pocket."

"You mean a repair," said the man.

"Not a repair exactly…" Albert started to reply.

"Grandad!" called out the young man. "You got a guy out here asking about a watch repair."

An old man shuffled out of the back. "We've talked about this, Johnny. You know how to examine a watch. How are you going to take over this place if you don't start doing things for yourself?"

The young man just sighed and continued reading his magazine. The old man smacked him in the back of the head. "Go put on some coffee," the old man ordered him.

"Alright, alright," said the young man rubbing his head. He went into the back.

"Ladies and gentlemen….the future," the old man called after him. "Isn't it bright?" He shook his head and apologized to Albert.

"Now what can I help you with?" he asked.

Albert handed over the old watch. "I wanted to see if you knew anything about this watch or the inscription."

"Let's take a look," replied the old man as Albert handed him the watch. He held it up to an eye piece that had been hanging around his neck.

"Nice piece," he said. "A very nice piece. I see you've got it working again. With some more care it could be almost like new."

"Do you know where it came from?" asked Albert.

"Might have come from here," said the old man. "I sold a lot of these in my day."

"Do you recognize the inscription?" asked Albert.

"It seems familiar," replied the old man. "I inscribed a lot of watches. My memory isn't the same these days."

"How old is it?" asked Albert.

"Looks about fifty-three or fifty-four," said the old man. He handed the watch back to Albert. "Wish I could tell you more. Nice piece, though."

"I found it along a path in the woods. I'd like to get it back where it belongs," said Albert.

"Well it found its way to you," said the old man. "Maybe it's already where it belongs."

20

"Well that was rather unsatisfying," said the wallet.

"For once I have to agree," said the reading glasses. "I was hoping the jeweler would know more about the watch."

"Me too," said Albert. He was cooking dinner, using the stove this time.

"You'll feel better after a good home cooked meal," said the stove. "Better check those mushrooms," it added.

Albert stirred the mushrooms and added a bit more olive oil to them. "I wonder if there's someone else you could talk to about it.," he said.

"Not another wild goose chase," protested the wallet. "Do you know how much gas you wasted on that trip?"

"That's the farthest you've gone in months," said the keys. "Maybe you should talk to other jewelers."

"You could always make some calls," suggested the cell phone.

"I'm not really a phone person," said Albert.

"I know that," said the cell phone.

"Don't worry about it," said the stove. "Everything always looks better after a good meal."

"That's your answer to everything," said the wallet. "Happy, sad, confused, angry…just eat."

"And what is your answer to everything?" asked the stove.

"Careful planning," said the wallet. "Attention to details."

"You get too caught up in the details," said the keys. "Sometimes you need to just get out there and do things. Even though we didn't learn much it was still worth the trip."

"I agree," said the cell phone. "Talking to people…communication. That's the key to everything."

"Those are all good strategies," said the reading glasses. "But the most important thing is just to keep at it and be consistent in your efforts."

"What do you think, Albert?" asked the stove.

Albert shrugged. He finished cooking and sat down to eat. He put on his reading glasses and opened a book about plants. Albert stared at the illustrations and scientific names. The scientific names were always his favorite part.

He thought about the possibility of discovering a new plant. Albertus floravitus. He decided that had a nice ring to it. The idea and the book only held his attention for a few moments, however.

Albert took another bite and stared at the watch for a moment. He reread the inscription. "For TM. Much appreciation and good fortune." Who was TM? What had he or she done to receive the appreciation of a nice watch?

He listened to the watch but heard only the tick-tick-tick of its gears and hands. Apparently it had already said everything it intended.

"Not much of a talker, that watch," said the cell phone.

"You might take a lesson from that," said the wallet.

"An evening meal is no place for bickering," said the stove.

"I have to disagree," said the cell phone. "I'm sure there's a long history of bickering at the dinner table."

Albert just shook his head. There didn't seem to be much point in going from one place to another in search of information about the watch. Nor did it seem like a good idea to simply call random jewelry stores about it.

He thought that perhaps the old man was right. It was where it was meant to be…at least for now. He put watch down and continued reading his book on plants.

PART 2

1

This time the hostess recognized Albert as he walked into the restaurant. "Welcome back,"she said. "Are you dining alone or meeting someone today?"

"At least she didn't assume we were eating alone," said the cell phone.

"Looking for a good tip no doubt," said the wallet.

"That doesn't even make sense," replied the cell phone. "She's the hostess, not our waitress."

"They all share the tips these days," said the wallet.

"I'm meeting someone today," Albert interjected, putting an end to the debate.

"The editor is already here," said the reading glasses. "He's sitting there by the window." Albert's editor was waving his hand, gesturing for him to come over.

"It looks like he's found you," said the hostess. "I'll take you over." She escorted Albert over to the table. Albert nodded to the print of The Scream as he passed by it.

"Hello Albert," said the painting.

Albert's editor stood up and shook his hand as he reached the table. "Thanks for coming," he said. "I know you usually like to meet at your house but this is a special occasion – a truly great assignment. Plus I don't mind buying you lunch once in awhile."

"Thank you," said Albert. "But it's really not necessary. I like my work."

"I know you do," said the editor. "That's partly why you're so good at it. That and you work hard. And now that hard work has paid off."

They had to pause the conversation for a moment while the waitress took their drink order. After she left, the editor took a folder out of his briefcase.

"Here it comes," said the wallet.

"Relax," said the keys. "He already said it was a great assignment."

"Great for whom?" asked the wallet.

"Let's just hear the man out," said the reading glasses. "No reason to jump to conclusions."

The editor opened the folder and took out several pieces of paper. On top was a color brochure for a recreational vehicle, the kind you drove. Albert had heard them referred to as motor homes or coaches.

"We've been hired to write the manual for the new model of the Venture. And I knew we had to put our best man on it."

A chill went down Albert's spine and he turned to look at The Scream. The painting said nothing. It didn't have to say anything. It's permanent expression was enough.

"You will be the first one to experience the new model," continued the editor. "This brochure is just a proof copy. No one outside of the manufacturer has driven or stayed in one of these."

"I have to drive it?" asked Albert.

"Of course," replied the editor. "Drive it, sleep in it, travel in it. The manufacturer wants the manual to be practical and above all authentic. They want you to experience the motor coach."

"I don't think…." Albert protested.

"Albert," replied the editor. "You are my best writer and this is an important contract for the company. This is no coffeemaker." He leaned in closer. "And you deserve this. You need this. In all the years we've worked together I've never known you to take a vacation – a real vacation, not just time between assignments."

Albert didn't know what to say. "I just don't know if this is the best assignment for me," he said. "I'm not much of a traveler."

"That's exactly the idea behind this model," said the editor. "It's designed for first time owners, people who don't have previous experience with a motor coach."

Albert let out a long sigh.

"Tell him no," said the wallet. "Tell him you won't do it. You're not even remotely prepared for this type of assignment."

"Nonsense," said the keys. "It's perfect for you Albert, just like the editor said."

"Yes," agreed the cell phone. "Get out there, see things and meet people."

"Albert?" asked the editor. "What do you say?"

Albert opened his mouth to say something but nothing came out. He looked at the pictures of the motor coach on the brochure.

"It looks nice," said the cell phone.

"It's self-contained," said the keys. "Like taking your home with you."

"This is insane," objected the wallet. "This is not a decision to be made lightly."

Albert listened for the reading glasses, who had said nothing so far. He took them off and stared at them. Then he put them back a on and looked at the brochure through the lenses.

"You should do it," they said at last. "It's your assignment and you've never turned one down or left one incomplete."

Albert set his reading glasses on the table and looked up at the editor. He nodded.

2

Albert surveyed the already vast collection of materials he had collected on the kitchen table. He had started compiling materials on his desk but quickly outgrew that space.

Albert had amassed a wide assortment of road maps, travel brochures and two types of navigational compasses. He'd also downloaded two different mapping programs on his phone and printed out countless pages from the Internet.

"You have to get this organized," said the wallet. "At least start some piles. Put all the travel advisories over there."

"Do we really need all this?" asked the keys. "One of those print outs is a travel advisory about Manila . Are we driving the coach to Manila?"

"A little planning never hurt anyone," said the reading glasses.

"I don't think you need any of this," said the keys. "It's all just confusing."

"Maybe you should talk to a travel agent," suggested the cell phone.

"That's not a bad idea," said the reading glasses.

Albert shuffled the papers around the table a bit. "Maybe if I just started to remove the items I don't need," he said.

He picked up the advisory. "I probably won't need this," said Albert. He decided to read the document, expecting to confirm his decision. Albert's brow began to wrinkle as he read it. "It seems like these things could happen anywhere, not just Manila. This is full of good tips. I think I should keep it."

Albert put the travel advisory back on its pile and continued to look through the maps, brochures and documents. "All of this could be important," he said. He went back to his office for supplies and returned with folders, envelops, paper clips and highlighters.

Albert read through all the various materials. He took meticulous notes and highlighted passages on almost every document. He traced routes on the maps and circled key points of interest. After finishing with a document or print out he would file it with similar ones. Each collection was then placed in an accordion file.

The entire process took several hours. At one point Albert had to stop to eat. There was no room on the kitchen table so he had to stand over the kitchen sink.

"Slippery slope," said the stove. "You're on a slippery slope."

"Not even I can defend you on this one, Albert," said the microwave.

After eating, Albert continued to review and organize the materials. The sun had long gone down when he finally finished. He looked at the clock and realized this was the latest he'd stayed up in a very long time.

Everything was neatly organized, annotated and placed in a slot in the accordion file. Albert took a moment to reflect on everything he'd learned from the travel materials.

"Nothing," he said. "I've learned nothing. I'm no closer to figuring out where or how I should go then I was after lunch.

"I don't think you need to know where you are going," said the keys. "You should just go."

"That's a sure way to get lost," said the wallet.

"Sometimes getting lost isn't a bad thing," said the cell phone.

"Getting lost is never a good thing," said the reading glasses.

Albert realized he had a headache. He put the accordion folder aside and took some aspirin. One thing he knew for sure, it was very late and he was tired. Albert decided to go to bed.

Once in bed though, he was unable to sleep. He kept thinking about the motor coach and the impending trip. Visions of the various maps and brochures floated through his head.

This one seemed too far…that one might cost too much money. One destination might be too rough for the motor coach. Another might be too crowded this time of year. Plus he wondered just how he was expected to use the coach anyway. If he used it too little and the manual might not be authentic enough for the manufacturer. If he used it too much, he might place too much wear on it.

"Go see a travel agent, Albert," suggested the cell phone again.

"Maybe you should," said the reading glasses.

"I see dollar signs," said the wallet.

"You always see dollar signs," said the phone.

"I'll sleep on it," Albert finally decided. He closed his eyes just as the neighbor's car alarm began going off.

3

"Excuse me sir," said a voice to Albert's left. "Can I have a moment of your time?" Albert looked over to see a thermostat perched on top of a large plastic display.

"Yes?" asked Albert.

"What temperature is your house?" asked the thermostat.

"I can't say," said Albert. "I think I might have it set at seventy-two."

"If you had the HelloHome 400, you would know your exact temperature and humidity," explained the thermostat. "You could also change the temperature or program a future change of temperature from anywhere using your phone."

"Oh," said Albert. It had never occurred to him that he needed that type of control over the temperature of his house.

"Just keep walking," said the wallet in a hushed voice.

"People who use the HelloHome 400 typically save twenty to thirty percent on their utility bill every year," said the thermostat.

"Move on," said the wallet. "Did you make eye contact? You should never make eye contact."

Albert nodded. He started to walk away from the display.

"Don't you like saving money?" asked the thermostat.

"I....I do," said Albert.

"Don't you want to save twenty to thirty percent off your utility bill?" continued the thermostat.

"How much do you cost?" asked Albert. It was the first thing that popped into his mind.

"The HelloHome 400 pays for itself in just two years of savings," said the thermostat.

"Okay," said Albert. He stood awkwardly in front of the display.

"Would you like to schedule assistance with your installation?" asked the thermostat.

"I'm not sure I can afford it," replied Albert.

"The installation assistance?" asked the thermostat.

"The thermostat," said Albert.

"It pays for itself in two years," said the thermostat.

"Oh," said Albert. There was another awkward silence. "I'm not sure what that means," said Albert finally.

"The HelloHome 400 is just $599," said the thermostat. "Installation is another $199."

"It's a thermostat," said the wallet. "You can buy one for $30 in the next aisle."

"This is a smart thermostat," explained the thermostat. "It makes your home smarter."

"I see," said Albert.

"Don't you want a smart home?" asked the thermostat.

Albert thought about this for a moment. "What does that mean?" He asked.

"It means your home is smart enough to talk to your cell phone," said the thermostat.

"They talk every day," said Albert. "This morning they had an argument about the number of outlets."

The thermostat's display panel flashed what appeared to be an eye roll at Albert. "I mean talk electronically," it said.

"Uh huh," said Albert. He looked around nervously, trying to find an excuse to walk away from the display.

"You're not going to buy one, are you?" asked the thermostat. Albert could tell it was becoming annoyed with him.

"I don't think so," said Albert. "I'm sorry. I just don't think I need it. I don't leave the house that much."

"Oh well then you probably don't need it," quipped the thermostat.

"Okay then," said Albert. He nodded politely and started to to walk away.

"It will probably be too warm or cold when you get home," the thermostat shouted after him.

Once outside, Albert noticed the travel agency a few storefronts away. He walked over and went inside. A man at the counter took Albert's named and explained that he'd be with him in a moment.

"No one could be that excited to work in a travel agency," said the wallet.

"Just give him a chance," urged the reading glasses.

"Thanks for stopping in today…Allen was it?" asked the man a short time later.

"Albert," he replied.

"Of course, Albert," said the travel agent. "It's great to meet you, Albert. We're going to plan you a great trip." The man took out a pen and notebook. "So where would you like to go?"

"I don't know," said Albert. "I was hoping you could help me."

"Oh," said the pleasant young man. "Most people seem to already know where they would like to go. I mean at least they have an idea."

"See," gloated the wallet. "I told you this guy can't help. You're probably off script with him already."

The young man took a card out his pocket and stared at it for a moment. Then he flipped it over and stared at the other side. He opened his mouth to start talking but then seemed to think better of it.

"I'm sorry," said Albert. "I think this may have been a mistake."

The travel agent looked up. "Not at all," he said. He put the card in his desk. "There's no wrong way to take a vacation. Tell me some of the things you like to do in your spare time."

"I like to spend time at my house. I especially like to cook," said Albert.

"Let's focus on activities outside of your house," said the travel agent. "What do you like to do outside?"

Albert thought for a moment. "I like to take nature walks."

"Now there's something," said the travel agent. "Where do you usually walk?"

"A park near my home," said Albert. "They have a wooden path and a flower meadow."

The travel agent scribbled a few notes. "Do you think you'd like to visit other parks?"

Albert had never considered this idea. He liked the park by his house. He knew the direction of the paths, the exact number of steps and he always enjoyed the scenery.

"I don't know," Albert said honestly.

"A park is a park," said the keys. "How about a change in scenery?"

"He doesn't need a change in scenery," retorted the wallet.

"You mean you don't need a change in scenery," said the keys.

"Okay, let's approach this a different way," said the travel agent. "How do you like to travel?"

"I don't really like to travel," replied Albert.

The travel agent stared at him. "Unfortunately I don't have any brochures about your house Albert, but I can give you a route to get back home. I'll mark the gas stations and good places to eat along the way."

Albert was unsure what to say. "I think he was joking," explained the reading glasses.

The travel agent smiled and Albert chuckled. "I'm sorry," he said. "I have to travel for work. I'm writing a manual about a motor coach. They want me to use it for a trip."

The travel agent scribbled some notes. "Now that makes sense," he said. "So you'll be traveling by recreational vehicle…and we know that you like nature walks."

"Yes," confirmed Albert.

"I knew this was a good idea," said the cell phone. The wallet just grumbled in Albert's pocket.

"Wait here a moment," said the travel agent. "I think I have an idea." The travel agent left Albert sitting at the desk while he went over to a rack with maps and brochures. Then he went over to a computer and printed out some pages. The travel agent put everything together into a folder before bringing it back over to Albert.

The travel agent opened the folder and set in before Albert. "The National Park system," he said. "This is the trip for you. They have nature walks and can accommodate recreational vehicles. And they're located all over…near and far."

Albert looked through the brochures and route maps. He saw pictures of meadows and mountains. There were photos of motor coaches right in the parks. One of the parks had several waterfalls. He held it up to the travel agent. "I think I'd like to see these waterfalls," said Albert.

"I think the manufacturer would like this," said the reading glasses. "It's the perfect kind of trip for the manual. And it doesn't seem too hard."

"I vote yes," said the keys.

"Me too," added the cell phone.

"Seems like you're rushing in," said the wallet. "I recommend you take some time to think about this."

Albert looked at the travel materials for another few minutes. "I think this could work," he said finally. "I think I can do this."

4

Albert found his brother sitting at their usual table in the restaurant.

"How are you, Albert?" asked his brother.

"I'm fine," replied Albert. "How are you?"

"I'm doing well," said his brother. "The new job is coming along and Jane is really whipping the school board into shape."

"That sounds very exciting," said Albert.

"No it doesn't," objected the poster of the Munch painting in the restaurant. "Does he always talk about the same things?"

Albert nodded to the painting and his brother. "Talking about himself," continued the painting. 'It is his favorite topic." Albert gave the painting a look of disapproval.

"Are you keeping busy?" asked Albert's brother.

"Yes," said Albert. "I actually just got a new assignment."

"Another coffeemaker?" asked his brother. "Perhaps a refrigerator this time?"

"It's a motor coach," said Albert. He took the brochure for the Venture out his pocket and unfolded it.

"You mean like a camper?" asked his brother. "The ones you drive?"

Albert slid the brochure across the table. His brother picked it up and looked it over. "I don't know about this," he said. He rubbed the burn scar on his cheek.

It's a big assignment," said Albert with pride. "They want me to travel around in it and write the manual."

"Albert, this machine is really large, with lots of complicated parts," said his brother. "And you'll have to drive it and take care of it."

"Yes," said Albert. The manufacturer wants me to use it. To keep the manual authentic."

His brother folded the brochure and put it back down on the table. "Listen Albert, you know I would like to see you do something more than just write manuals. But at least writing manuals is mostly safe work. I think you may be biting off more than you can chew this time."

Albert looked down at the brochure. All of a sudden the motor coach did look extremely large and complicated.

"Isn't there something less complicated you can write about?" asked his brother. "Something you don't have drive and park? An electric tooth brush or a board game?"

"My editor wants me to do it," replied Albert. "He recommended me."

"How are you going to travel around in this?" asked his brother. "You don't like to leave the house or go new places. You always want to meet at this same restaurant and you always order the same thing."

The waitress brought their food. For Albert that always meant a classic wedge salad with grilled chicken on the side. He liked this restaurant because they always put the dressing on the side and separated the lettuce and the other elements of the salad.

Albert looked down at his salad and then at the brochure for the Venture. "It is large," he said. "And I had a lot of trouble deciding where to go."

"But you did decide," protested the painting. "Show him the brochures on the parks."

"Now you're making some sense," said his brother. "Why don't you call your editor and tell you him can't do it. See if he has another assignment."

"Don't listen to him," said the painting. "Last time you were here he told you to get a hobby. Tell him camping is your new hobby."

"Maybe camping can be my new hobby," said Albert.

"Albert stop talking nonsense," said his brother. "The last thing you need is to be distracted by hobbies."

"But..." Albert stammered.

"You have to talk to your editor," said his brother.

"He thought it might be good for me," said Albert.

"Then you're editor doesn't know you well," said his brother. "He doesn't have your best interest in mind."

"He probably knows you better than your own brother," interjected the painting.

Albert let out a long sigh. "I was thinking it might be good for me," said Albert.

"Then you don't know yourself very well," replied his brother. "This is beyond your scope. You'll end up lost in the woods somewhere. And then I'll have to come find you."

His brother shook his head and got up from the table. "I'll be right back," he said. Albert looked down and picked at his food.

"Just ignore him, Albert," said the painting.

"He is my brother," said Albert. "And he has his reasons."

"Your brother is a hypocrite,"said the painting. "I see his kind all the time. He acts like he's always taking on new challenges but he never strays from his own comfort zone. He makes me so mad I want to…well, you know."

"At least he's safe," said Albert. "And he tries to help me stay safe."

Albert took out the brochures of the parks and looked them over. He was worried but a part of him really did want to see those places. After a few moments his brother returned and they finished their meals in silence. Without a word his brother signaled for the waitress and paid the check.

"I have to get back to work," he said getting up from the table. "Think about what I've said, Albert. Think about the day at the beach when we were kids. You know I don't like to bring that up, but…"

Albert started to reply then closed his mouth and lowered his eyes.

"You're just not good in certain situations, Albert," said his brother. He took a few steps back to the table. "Stick to what you know, Albert…like me. That's what I learned that day. And that's all I want to say about it."

"The beach or my trip?" asked Albert.

"All of it," his brother replied before walking away.

5

Albert was writing in mid-sentence when he suddenly felt himself drop several inches. His fingers were no longer level with the desk and he had to strain to type the last few words.

"What happened?" asked the reading glasses.

"The chair adjustment must have slipped," said Albert. He reached down the side of the chair and grabbed the adjustment lever. Pulling the lever up he took his weight off the chair and it rose back up.

"There you go," the chair said accommodatingly.

"That's better," said Albert. However, as he started to type he noticed that his fingers were now too high for the keyboard. He pulled the lever once again. The chair dropped back down to its lowest height.

"So sorry about that," said the chair.

Albert pulled the lever and shifted his weight to bring it up again. This time he didn't raise the chair as high. He started to type again, but he realized it still didn't seem right.

"That is the height you usually sit at," said the chair.

"Are you sure?" asked the reading glasses.

"Are you?" snapped the chair.

Albert pulled another lever on the chair and began to adjust the tilt of the chair. He moved forward and then back, each time trying to type again. Nothing seemed quite right.

"Albert," said the chair, "you're going to wear out the adjustments."

"It's not the same," said Albert.

"I have over one hundred different positions," said the chair. "It is unlikely you'll get back to the exact spot."

"But he's sat in that position for years," said the reading glasses. "It was the perfect height and angle for typing."

"I'm not sure there is one perfect height," said the chair. "They're all valuable in their own way."

Albert continued to adjust the chair as they spoke. The chair sunk down to it's lowest level again.

"Who would even want to sit at this height?" asked Albert. "I can't even reach the desk."

"It's perfect for dusting under the desk," explained the chair.

"That's not funny," said the reading glasses. "He needs to get back to work."

"So pick a different position," said the chair.

Albert continued to fiddle with the chair and eventually reached a position that was at least very close to his old one.

"See," said the chair. "This position is just as good."

Albert began typing and finished his current page. However, he didn't feel the same. He thought for a moment, tapping his fingers on the desk. Albert had an idea. He grabbed a magazine from the corner of the desk and placed it under his laptop. He tried typing again and discovered it was his previous position.

"You're welcome," said the chair.

"This will do for now," said Albert. "I may have to get a new chair tomorrow."

There was a knock at Albert's door. "Go see who it is," said the cell phone enthusiastically.

"It's the middle the afternoon," cautioned the wallet. "This is likely to be someone soliciting you. Be ready with your polite but firm dismissal."

"It's not good to jump to conclusions either way," said the reading glasses.

Albert made his way down the hallway and answered the door. The man on the other side was wearing the uniform of a transport company and holding a clipboard. After confirming Albert's name, he explained that he had a vehicle delivery for him.

"If you move your car we can put it in the driveway," said the delivery man.

"The driveway?" asked Albert.

"Yes," replied the delivery man. "Neighbors might complain if you leave it in the street."

"Okay," replied Albert. He went outside and moved the car from the driveway. Once he had parked in the street, the delivery man said something into a cell phone and Albert saw a large truck turn the corner and park by the house. The delivery man and a helper began removing the cover off a large vehicle on the truck.

The Venture had arrived. It was a painted a brilliant white accented with bright waves of color curving down from the top and across each side. Windows dominated the front of the motor coach and were in various shapes and sizes along the sides. The motor coach took up most of his driveway.

Taking a closer look, Albert saw a number of plugs, nozzles and storage doors along the bottom part of the coach. "That's…a lot," said Albert.

" I see you're already doing the walk around," said the delivery man. "Just let me know if you see any damage and I'll note it here. It all checked out when we picked it up but you should double check before you sign off."

"Better look close," warned the wallet. "We don't want to get blamed for any damage."

"It looks fine to me," said the keys. "Just sign the form so we can look inside."

"Here, I'll walk around with you," said the delivery man. "It's a beautiful machine. Wouldn't mind having one of these myself."

"I'm supposed to write the manual," said Albert as they circled the motor coach.

"Wow," said the delivery man. "Wish I had that job. Imagine being the first to try things out."

"This is my biggest assignment," said Albert, staring straight up at the Venture.

"I'm sure you'll have a ball," said the delivery man. "See anything?'

"What?" asked Albert.

"See any damage?" asked the delivery man.

"Oh," said Albert. "Everything looks fine."

"Great," replied the delivery man. "Sign here and we'll get out of your way."

Albert signed and the delivery man handed him the keys. "Registration and other paperwork is in the glove compartment. Have a great day." The delivery man got back in the truck and drove off, leaving Albert alone with the motor coach.

"Okay," said the car keys, "we've seen the outside. Why don't we take a look inside?"

Albert used the key the delivery man had given him to open the side door and enter the motor coach. Once inside he immediately noticed the smell. It was the smell of "new" – new wood, new cloth, new leather, new everything. The appliances and controls were even still covered in a plastic. There was a warning on each to remove it before use.

Albert looked around. The motor coach had everything you could want in a home. There was a couch, a television and a small kitchen that even had an oven. Down the hallway was a bathroom and a bedroom with a large bed, another television, closet and drawers. The whole thing felt self-contained and cozy. It was much smaller than his house of course, but nonetheless it felt sufficient and safe.

"See, Albert," said the keys. "It's like taking a mini-house with you wherever you go."

Albert walked to the front of the motor coach. Two leather chairs sat in front of a host a dials, dashes, toggles and screens. Albert had never been in an airplane cockpit, but he assumed it might look something like this.

"All the comforts of home and you can take it anywhere," said the keys.

"If I can figure out how to work all this," said Albert.

"I see a steering wheel, gas pedal, brake and gauges," replied the keys. "Same as the car, just a little bigger."

"Never mind that," said the wallet. "This is much more complicated than the car. Albert, you've got a lot to figure out if you're going to operate this machine."

Albert touched a button and a load air horn suddenly went off. "I certainly do," said Albert.

6

"Yes, I'm still holding," said Albert.

"Please continue holding," said the voice on the other line. "He is currently traveling you know."

"I didn't know that," said Albert.

"Yes," said the voice. "He's visiting some of the satellite offices. He'll be away for almost a month."

"He didn't tell me," said Albert.

"I can send you to his voice mail if you'd like," said the voice.

"No, thank you," replied Albert. "I'll just try again later." He hung up the phone. Albert disliked leaving voice mails even more than he disliked talking on the phone.

"You weren't able to talk to him?" asked the wallet.

"No," said Albert. "He's traveling."

"Isn't that just perfect," said the wallet. "He's not available and you have that monstrosity in the driveway. You should have turned down this assignment in the first place."

"You should make the best of it," said the keys.

"I agree," said the reading glasses.

"You agree?" said the wallet.

"I would think you above anyone could clearly see the impracticality of this," said the wallet.

"Albert is consistent and reliable," explained the reading glasses. "This should be no different."

"I've never turned down an assignment," agreed Albert. "I'm just a bit overwhelmed. What if my brother is right?"

"He's not right, Albert," said the cell phone. "He doesn't understand anything about you."

"I didn't drink coffee before I wrote about the first coffeemaker manual," said Albert.

"And now it keeps you up at night," said the wallet.

"The car alarm keeps me up at night," said Albert.

"Then get away from it for awhile," said the keys.

"Walking away is your solution to everything," said the wallet.

Albert started to dial the editor's number again. He considered the wallet's last statement and stopped. "Not keeping the assignment is like walking away," he said. That idea gave Albert at least a degree of peace. He wasn't entirely happy about the assignment, but it was his assignment.

Albert walked outside the house and stood looking at the Venture for several moments. He went back inside the motor coach and walked around, placing his hands on the counter and walls. Albert ran his fingers over the various switches, dials and buttons. He opened the refrigerator and rummaged around the bins and drawers. Everything was silent. There didn't even seem to be any ambient noise.

"Maybe there's something wrong," wondered Albert.

"The wallet probably offended it," suggested the cell phone.

Albert sat down on the couch. He was feeling very tired so he laid down and stared up at the paneling on the ceiling. Albert found himself getting lost in the patterns in the wood. After a few moments they began to blur together and Albert drifted off to sleep.

He awoke several hours later in the dark. Albert tried to check the time on the old watch but it was too dark for that. Looking at his phone, he saw the late hour and realized he was hungry. Albert got up from the couch and stumbled around the motor coach. He didn't even know the locations of the light switches.

Albert held out his arms and felt along the walls until he was able to locate the door. He moved his hands around until he gripped the handle. Albert opened the door and almost tripped on his way out of the motor coach.

Albert went back inside the house and into the kitchen. He decided to make some pancakes. He put a pan on the stove and began making the batter.

"Like I said before," said the wallet, "if you're going to do this you will need to have a plan."

"I know," said Albert. "I'll have to figure something out."

Albert poured the batter into pan, making three nearly perfect discs. "It's like making pancakes," said the stove.

"What's like making pancakes?" asked the microwave.

"Using a motor coach," replied the stove. "You follow the recipe, make the batter and cook it. It's a series of steps and instructions. Complex instructions, but still instructions."

Albert gave the pancakes a final flip and put them a plate. He sat down at the table and poured the syrup. "I can make pancakes," he said between bites.

"You're great at making pancakes," said the stove. "Well shaped, crunch on the crust and soft in the middle."

Albert finished his meal. "I do make good pancakes," he said. He rinsed off his plate and went up to bed.

"You will still need a plan," said the wallet from its place on the nightstand.

"I know," said Albert. "But maybe it is all just a series of individual steps – just like any other manual."

7

Albert brought a pencil and notebook along with him on his nature walk. That was something he'd never done before. He normally preferred to walk without having to carry anything with him. However, he today thought he might make some notes and draw some sketches.

Albert made his way along the path, looking for interesting plants. After a few steps it occurred to him he wasn't actually sure what made a plant particularly interesting. He saw several that he liked of course, but none he would describe as interesting.

Still, the meadow path made him feel calm as always. He decided not to worry about sketching or taking notes on his first pass down the path. The weather was pleasant today – one of those rare days that wasn't too hot or too cold with only a slight breeze.

The path was busier than usual, most likely because of the good weather. Albert had to stop walking more than once to avoid crowds along the path. On one of these stops he couldn't help overhearing a conversation.

"This is an interesting one," said a woman to a man who Albert could only assume was her husband. "It has these little blue flowers on the end of the stem."

"I've never seen one quite like it," replied the man. "I'll take a picture so we can look it up when we get home."

"Maybe we can plant some by the front walk," said the woman. "As long as we can figure out the name of the plant."

The couple lingered a bit more and then continued down the path. Albert took out his notebook and pen as he took their place along the path. He was disappointed when he saw the blue flowers they had been talking about.

"These aren't interesting at all," he thought to himself. "These bloom by the path at this time every year. They're fairly common as a matter of fact."

He put the notebook away and continued walking. Albert was still behind the couple as they stopped to admire another example of fauna. "What a deep shade of green," observed the man.

"Yes," agreed the woman. They took another picture before moving on.

Albert went over to get a look. He was glad he hadn't bothered to take out his notebook this time. The plant was a simple fern.

"A fern," Albert thought to himself. "I have one of those at home. I've been trying to get rid of it for two years. It keeps spreading along my fence."

Albert was immediately angry with himself for being judgmental. It wasn't his place to be critical about other people's interest in plants. If they liked the little blue flowers and ferns it didn't matter whether or not they were interesting to Albert.

However, he did wish he had the path to himself. It occurred to Albert that he didn't usually go for nature walks on the weekend. That would be another reason the path was crowded. Albert realized just how much he was off his regular routine.

Luckily, the couple did not stop again and Albert was able to walk the rest of the path unimpeded. He had to follow right behind the same couple the rest of the way though.

They reached the end of the path and walked over to their car. Albert noticed the license plates were from out of state. They were most likely newcomers to the path. "That might explain their fascination with locally common plants," he thought.

Albert looked over at his own car and considered walking the path again. He decided against it. The crowds made the walk too unpleasant so he didn't see the point of extending the day. He got back his car and set his notebook on the seat.

Albert picked the notebook back up and leafed through it. It was blank except for the words "Interesting Plants" and the date written and underlined on the first page. Albert put the book in the glove compartment and drove home.

8

"Honestly Albert," said the car keys, "I don't know why you spend so much time going through all of this."

"You never know," said the wallet. "Sometimes there's a valuable coupon in here. It pays to be thorough."

"And Albert enjoys this," added the reading glasses.

Albert nodded. He did enjoy going through the flyers, advertisements and other junk mail. The activity usually represented his afternoon break. He would stop working at precisely two-fifty in the afternoon, a few minutes before the mail arrived. Albert would watch the truck come and go before going out to retrieve the mail. Then he sat at the kitchen table going through it.

He divided everything into three neat piles. The first pile contained items he planned to throw away after he was done. The second pile contained items he intended to use right away such as a coupon or other discount. The third pile contained items that he might need in the future.

"Twenty percent off carpet cleaning," announced one of the coupons.

"That's a good discount," said the wallet.

"Albert has hardwood floors," replied the car keys.

"That is true," said Albert. He placed the carpet coupon in the discard pile.

"Five dollars off any entrée," declared the next coupon. Albert placed it in the second pile.

"That restaurant has terrible reviews," said the cell phone.

"Is that a reason to throw away five dollars?" asked the wallet.

Albert picked the coupon back up. "Free soft drink refills," the coupon added.

"There you go," said the wallet.

"Everyone has free drink refills nowadays," said the car keys.

"Yes," said Albert. He continued to hold onto the coupon.

"Uh…kids eat free on Sundays?" suggested the coupon desperately.

"Albert doesn't have any children," said the reading glasses. "And he rarely eats out."

"Uh huh," agreed Albert. He started to put the coupon in the discard pile, then paused for a moment. He decided to put it in the future pile instead.

"I expire next week," came the final surly reply from the coupon. Albert scowled and moved the coupon to the discard pile.

Next in the stack was a request for donations from a local veteran's group. Albert placed that on the refrigerator using a magnet. After that he placed two more carpet cleaning coupons in the discard pile and a duct cleaning coupon in the future pile.

"Buy a dozen bagels, get six free," announced the next coupon. "Valid at Jacob's Bakery. Limit one per customer. Not valid with any other offers."

"I like bagels," said Albert.

"And you go to Jacob's almost once a week," added the reading glasses.

"See," said the wallet. "It is worth going through the coupons."

Albert finished going through the coupons and placed the items from the discard pile into the trash. Along the way he caught sight of the motor coach through the window.

"It's been almost two days now, Albert," said the car keys. "You need to either start writing about that thing or send it back."

"I'm sure he's just collecting his thoughts," said the reading glasses.

Albert nodded. He was figuring out the right way to tackle the assignment. Most of the time he wrote about one item at a time, but the motor coach was really a collection of many items. Albert reasoned he would have to explain each of them one at a time.

Albert retrieved the keys to the motor coach from the rack and walked out to the vehicle. He unlocked the Venture and went inside. He sat down in the drivers seat and inserted the key. After taking a deep breath, Albert turned the key and started the motor coach.

As the engine turned over the rest of the vehicle came to life. Screens and lights lit up, clocks and panels let out chirps and beeps. He heard the refrigerator kick on behind him.

"Not that different from turning on a coffeemaker," Albert said out loud.

"Just the same," said the cell phone. "Good job, Albert."

"All he did was start the engine," said the wallet.

"Oh, pipe down you," replied the cell phone.

Albert jotted down some notes and looked around the cab area. "The engine must be charging the batteries and supplying power. That's why everything is running now."

"Good thinking, Albert," said the reading glasses. "Start with the power systems."

"How about you drive it somewhere?" suggested the car keys. "You can turn on the lights and sit in a chair back in the house."

"One step at a time," said the wallet.

Albert reviewed the gauges around the drivers seat and took additional notes. "The Venture has several power indicators," he said. "They allow you to view the current state of the main battery as well as the auxiliary batteries."

He wrote these observations down and continued to work his way through the features around the driver's seat. Albert focused on one area at a time, learning everything he could about it before moving to the next.

"This is going to take forever," lamented the car keys. "Isn't there any way you can get through this quicker?"

"He can't rush this," replied the reading glasses. "It's important to get everything right and not to miss anything."

"Any chance you'll at least take this thing out for a quick spin?" asked the car keys.

Albert shook his head. "Not today," he said. "I have a lot to cover before I even think about that."

The car keys let out a huff. "The coach probably doesn't remember what it's supposed to do....it thinks it's just a storage pod."

"Always impatient," said the wallet. "Demanding to go here or go there. Advising to just get it done."

"Exactly," said the keys. "Get this rig rolling, Albert."

"That kind of thinking doesn't pay the bills," said the wallet.

"I think that's enough fighting for today," interjected the cell phone.

"I agree," said the reading glasses.

Albert continued writing down his thoughts. He moved on to the vehicle's Global Positioning System. "The Venture's Global Positioning System indicates your current location…"

"The driveway," interjected the keys. "It's sitting in the driveway."

"…and allows you to plot directions to any other location or address by typing or speaking into the unit," continued Albert.

"Anywhere but the driveway," said the keys. "Plot directions to anywhere but here."

"It also allows you to find nearby services and attractions such as restaurants, gas stations and recreational areas," said Albert.

"Sounds good," said the keys. "A nearby park, take out Chinese…whatever you've got."

"I don't think you're being very helpful," said the reading glasses.

"Just ignore him" said the wallet. "He's never happy unless we're moving."

"Moving forward," said the car keys. "Ask it the way forward, Albert."

Albert stopped what he was doing and thought about this. After a moment he leaned towards the navigation screen and pressed the button to talk.

"The way forward," he said into the small microphone. "Tell me the way forward."

The navigation was blank and quiet at first, as though it were thinking. After a short time it responded, "Here are some possible matches for 'way forward'."

Albert was elated. He couldn't believe it was that easy to get an answer to such a question…until he read the results. The system had simply returned anything nearby with the words "way" or "forward." There were several streets called this or that "way" and a few businesses such as Forward Thinking Advertising, Inc.

Disappointed, Albert cleared the screen. "I suppose it was worth a try," he said.

"You have to answer that question for yourself," replied the motor coach in a deep voice.

9

"Be careful Albert," said the bicycle. "Don't drop me. You'll scratch my paint. Or worse…I could break."

"I've got it," said Albert as he removed the bicycle from its hooks. In truth, he felt very unbalanced and regretted not moving the box of recyclables further away before lifting the bike.

"I think I'm slipping," said the bicycle.

The bicycle started to tilt over, it's fall stopped only by the wall of the garage. Albert shifted the bike's weight and managed to set the bicycle down on the floor.

"That was very strenuous and stressful Albert," said the bicycle. "That probably covers your cardio for the day. You can probably skip the ride for today."

"I'm fine," said Albert. "And it's a nice day for a bike ride." Albert pressed the button to raise the garage door.

"It looks like rain," said the bicycle.

"There's hardly a cloud," said Albert. He got on the bicycle and peddled down the driveway.

"Careful," said the bicycle. "Don't hit that monstrosity in the driveway."

Albert maneuvered the bike along the side of the motor coach. He had to put out his hand a couple of times but managed to make it past the vehicle without running into it or scraping it.

"There we go," said Albert as he headed down the street. "Nice and easy. It's been awhile since I've ridden but it's just like...well you know."

"Maybe if you rode more often," said the bike, "we'd both feel a bit better."

"I might ride a lot more in the campground," said Albert.

"Campground?" asked the bicycle. "You mean in the woods?"

"Yes," said Albert.

"On dirt roads? Possibly even grass?" protested the bicycle.

"Probably dirt roads," confirmed Albert.

"I am designed for flat surfaces," said the bicycle. The bike bounced violently over a patch in the road as if to emphasize this point.

"The salesman said you were more of a hybrid," said Albert.

"Of course he did," said the bicycle. "He was trying to sell you a bicycle."

Albert rode in silence for awhile. He circled around the neighborhood several times before heading back down his own street. The motor coach came into view about a half a block away.

"Just a minute," said the bicycle. "How are you getting me to the campground? Are you going to tie me up there on the roof? You know I don't like heights."

"There's a rack on the back," said Albert. He gestured towards the rear of the motor coach as they reached the driveway.

"You're strapping me to rear of that thing?" The bicycle replied indignantly. "I'm a finely tuned machine. It's bad enough you hang me up on those hooks."

"It's very secure," said Albert. "I wrote the instructions the other day."

"Maybe I should just stay home," said the bicycle. "You'll probably be too busy to ride anyway."

"I should have time," said Albert.

"I'll be fine here," said the bicycle. "Just leave me on the hooks."

"I thought you didn't like the hooks," said Albert.

"I love the hooks," said the bicycle. "I can see everything from up there."

Albert hung up the bicycle and went back in the house. He went upstairs to the bathroom and took another look at the items he'd laid earlier that day. He had his toothbrush, toothpaste, razor, shaving cream and deodorant. He'd lined up each item on a towel he'd set on the counter.

Albert rolled the items up in the towel and walked out of the bathroom and into the bedroom. On the bed were his pillow and favorite blanket. Albert's most comfortable robe was hanging on the closet door. He gathered everything up and placed it carefully into a small duffle bag.

He carried that duffle bag into the motor coach and immediately unpacked everything into the bathroom and bedroom areas. He checked everything one last time to make sure he hadn't forgotten anything.

Albert decided he was ready. He turned out the light and got into bed. At first he simply laid awake, listening to the different sounds. Albert could hear crickets chirping in the background and what he thought might even be a frog. There was also a low hum Albert assumed was the refrigerator.

The bed itself was more comfortable than he expected. It was nearly the same size as his bed in the house. The mattress was a bit harder than what he was used to but not necessarily in a bad way. In fact it wasn't long before Albert drifted off to sleep, thinking about the woods.

Almost immediately he was awoken by the sound of the car alarm. "It's even louder out here," said the reading glasses.

"This is what happens when you camp in the driveway," said the car keys.

"I don't know if this is what the manufacturer meant by experiencing the motor coach," said the cell phone.

"I believe that all of the systems of this vehicle function the same regardless of where it's parked," said the wallet.

"Why do you think there are wheels on this thing?" asked the car keys. "It's not a guest house."

"Any further away and I might not have power," said the clock radio. "How would Albert know what time to get up?"

"I suppose I could just sleep in," said Albert.

"I have an alarm," the cell phone reminded him.

"Must you take everyone's job?' asked the clock radio. "Don't forget your battery must be charged."

"Albert rarely makes calls," replied the cell phone. "My battery lasts a long time."

"Since you're here Albert," said the car keys, "Maybe you should build a fire in the front yard."

"That is out of the question," said the wallet.

"I believe that was a joke," the reading glasses explained to the wallet.

"It's hard to tell these days," said the wallet. "Two months ago I wouldn't have predicted Albert would be sleeping in a motor coach parked in the driveway."

"Don't be such a spoiled sport," said the cell phone.

"I suppose it could be worse," said the wallet. "This could be a tent."

Albert got up to get a glass of water. In addition to the electric he'd also hooked up the water and filled the tank. "No running water in a tent," he said.

He sat down on the bed and tapped the button on the clock to turn off the alarm program. "What about getting up in the morning?" protested the clock.

"I've decided to sleep in," said Albert. "After all, I am camping."

"In the driveway," added the car keys.

The car alarm continued to go off in the distance, "Do you think you should say something?" asked the cell phone.

"We could just drive down there," suggested the car keys.

"I don't want to be that guy," replied Albert. He rolled over and covered his head with an extra pillow.

10

Albert checked the gauges on the motor coach and adjusted the mirrors.

"That is the third time you've adjusted those mirrors," said the car keys. Albert had put the motor coach keys on the same ring so they were hanging from the ignition.

"Just want to be sure," said Albert. He looked at each mirror again, trying to make sure he was seeing as much as possible in each view.

Albert decided the mirrors were okay and put his foot on the brake pedal and his hand on the gear shift. "Here we go," he said. He started the move the gear shift then stopped. "I'd better check the lights."

"I'm sure you already checked the lights," said the keys.

Albert flipped on the headlights and one of the turn signals before getting out of the motor coach. He walked to the front of the vehicle. The lights were working. Albert walked to the front corner to observe the turn signal blinking and then checked the back. "Looks good," he concluded.

Albert got back into the cab. "Are we going now?" asked the keys. Albert didn't answer. Instead he turned off the one turn signal and turned on the other. Then he got out and checked the other signal.

"If I had eyes I'd be rolling them," called out the keys.

Albert returned to the cab once again and turned off the turn signal and headlights. After thinking a moment he turned the headlights back on. "Can't hurt to have the headlights on," he said.

"Good thinking," said the reading glasses.

"I'm just not sure you'll pass any other cars here in the driveway," said the keys. "On or off doesn't make much difference."

"No patience as usual," said the wallet.

"He's just being cautious," said the reading glasses.

Albert put his foot back on the brake pedal and a worried look came over his face. "What is it, Albert?" asked the cell phone.

"The brake lights," said Albert. "How do I know if the brake lights are coming on?"

"That's why it's good to have a traveling companion, Albert," said the cell phone.

Albert stared ahead at the garage and thought about the problem. He realized that if he was facing the other direction the brake lights would reflect off the white garage door. "I have to turn the motor coach around," he said.

Albert put his foot back on the brake pedal and put the gear shift into reverse. He took his foot slightly off the pedal and the vehicle began to roll backward.

"Finally some movement," said the keys.

Albert began to turn the steering wheel as the motor coach rolled out into the street. However, he started too late and the vehicle did not swing far enough to avoid the other curb. Albert shifted into forward and lightly pressed the accelerator. This time he turned the wheel quicker but still did not make much headway on the turn.

"This is going to take a very long time," concluded the keys.

"I'm just glad everyone has left for work," said the cell phone.

Albert repeated the process of going forward and back several more times. After about ten minutes he had managed to point the motor coach perpendicular to his driveway.

"This is exactly why I think you are in over your head, Albert," said the wallet.

"He's just being careful," said the reading glasses. "He's doing fine. Now you can back into the driveway, Albert."

This was easier said then done. Albert had to go back and forth several more times before he was able to angle the motor coach into the driveway. He backed up slowly until he heard a crunch.

"I believe that would be one of the driveway lights," said the wallet. "That will cost you eight dollars to replace."

Albert continued backward and heard another crunch. "Another eight dollars," said the wallet.

Albert sighed and pulled forward. He repositioned the vehicle and backed up again. This time he did a little better. Albert let out a sigh of relief as the rear of the coach finally reached the garage door.

He pumped the brake and looked in each side mirror. Albert smiled at the red glow reflecting off the garage door on either side. "The brake lights work," he announced.

"I can't imagine how the lawn must look," said the wallet.

"That's enough for today," announced Albert. "I'm going to write up some notes about backing up."

"Maybe you should research which parks have pull through sites," added the keys.

11

"You're checking the lights again?" asked the keys.

"He's just being careful," said the reading glasses. "This is a large vehicle."

Albert checked all the lights again and took his position behind the wheel. He backed down the driveway and turned the wheel sharply. Thus time Albert almost made it all the way. One of the front tires jumped the curb for a couple of feet before dropping back down on the street. The entire motor coach shook and shuddered.

"You're doing fine, Albert," said the car keys. "Keep going. No harm done."

Albert surprised himself a bit as he kept going and drove the motor coach down his street. He reached the end of the street, slowed down and put on his turn signal. Albert made a right turn and continued down the next street.

"Doing great," said the cell phone.

Albert smiled and kept going. He reached the next street and made another right turn. A short distance later, Albert made yet another right turn. This brought him past his house again. He was feeling more comfortable so he continued further. Albert turned right again at the end of the street.

"Albert, are you trying out for UPS?" asked the keys. "That steering wheel turns both ways, you know."

Albert had come all the way to his house yet again and he drove on to the end of the street. "Left turn...left turn," chanted the car keys. The cell phone joined in as well.

"I think you're ready for a left," said the reading glasses.

At the last moment, Albert switched on the other turn signal and went left. He turned too wide and jumped the curb on the other side. The motor coach lurched upward again. Albert kept going and the wheel dropped back onto street.

"See, that wasn't so bad," said the keys.

Albert smiled and continued down the road. He was doing well until a squirrel suddenly darted out in front of him. Albert slammed on the brakes and watched the squirrel run out of the way. For a moment the squirrel looked up at Albert. He was sure the squirrel appeared angry with him.

He heard a loud honk behind him. Albert looked in the side mirror and saw a small white car there. Shaken, he pulled the motor coach over to the side of the street. The car honked again before darting out and passing him on the left side. As it went by, Albert made eye contact with the driver. He seemed to have the same look as the squirrel.

Albert put the motor coach in park and sat there for a few moments. "Shake it off," suggested the cell phone. Albert was shaking, but not in a way that made himself feel better. He got up from the driver's seat and went back to the bathroom. The tanks were still filled so he was able to splash some water on his face.

Albert looked in the mirror. Instead of his own reflection he saw the face of his brother. "This is too much for you, Albert" he said. "Go back to writing about coffeemakers."

The reflection changed the driver of the little white car. "Get off the road," said the driver. "That's too much vehicle for you."

Now the face of the driver changed to the head of the squirrel. "Are you nuts or something?" asked the squirrel.

Albert shook his head vigorously and the face in the mirror changed back to his own. "Am I nuts?" he asked himself. "Is this too much for me?"

"Only you can answer those questions," said the deep voice.

"You keep saying that," said Albert. He grabbed a towels and wiped his face. Albert returned to the driver's seat. He put the motor coach back in gear and drove back to his house. At the foot of the driveway he stopped and took the motor coach out of gear.

"Only you can answer those questions," said the deep voice again.

Albert put the motor coach back in gear and pulled forward past the house. He switched to reverse and carefully backed the vehicle into the driveway. Albert had to re-align it a few times, but he made it in without digging into the lawn or crushing any more lights.

12

Albert woke up craving a bagel. Looking out the window he saw it was a clear day – a good day for a drive to the bakery downtown. He remembered that he even had a coupon.

Albert gathered up his keys, wallet, phone and glasses. He locked up the house and started down the front walk to his car. With the motor coach taking up most of the driveway, he was parking the car in the street.

Albert looked back at the motor coach. "What are you thinking?" asked the wallet.

Albert looked at his keys. He held up the key to the car, then the one for the motor coach. "Albert, have you forgotten about the incident with the squirrel?" objected the wallet.

"Don't listen, Albert," said the keys. "Get right back on that horse."

"There won't room to park that thing," protested the wallet.

It had been three days since Albert drove the coach around the neighborhood. Since that time he had documented several more of its systems and slept inside twice. However, he had not driven it again.

"Today seems like a good day for a drive," Albert said.

"In the car," clarified the wallet.

"In the motor coach," replied the keys. "You'll be fine Albert."

"Maybe just skip the left turns," added the reading glasses.

Albert got into the motor coach and sat down in the driver's seat. He put the key in the ignition. "Is it a good day for a drive?" he wondered aloud.

"Only you can decide," said the deep voice.

Albert turned the key and started the motor coach. He put the vehicle in drive and started down the driveway. He turned to the right and headed for the downtown area. Albert navigated the motor coach to the block with the bakery without incident.

Once there, he needed to find someplace to park the coach. The downtown area by Albert's home wasn't large – only a few blocks – but it stayed relatively busy, especially in the morning. Albert came to a stop in front of the bakery and looked around. The two spaces immediately in front of the bakery were filled. There was a blank spot by the next storefront but Albert needed two spaces to accommodate the Venture.

"I told you this was a bad idea," said the wallet. "You'll never find a place to park this monstrosity. Honestly, I don't know what you were thinking."

There was a loud honk behind Albert and he started to doubt himself. "I guess I should drive home," said Albert. "A bowl of cereal will be fine."

There was a knock at the window. A shudder ran through Albert as he looked over. The baker was outside the window. He smiled and waved at Albert. Albert rolled down the window.

"Good morning, Albert," said the baker. "That's quite a rig you have here."

"Thank you…good morning, Jacob," said Albert. "I was thinking a bagel would sound good for breakfast today."

There was another loud honk from behind the motor coach. The baker looked back and gestured for the driver to settle down. "Hold your horses," called the baker. "Albert, why don't you pull around the back and park in the delivery area. I'll toast you up a fresh bagel."

"Okay," replied Albert.

The car behind him honked again. "What's your hurry?" shouted the baker. "Coffee, Albert?"

"Yes, please," said Albert.

"All right then," said the baker. "You pull around back and I'll see you inside."

13

"How did the parking go?" asked the baker when Albert walked into the bakery.

"Fine," replied Albert. "Thank you." It had gone fairly well actually. He'd had to jostle back and forth a few times but he'd gotten the motor coach parked without much trouble.

The baker gestured for Albert to have a seat and brought him his bagel and coffee. "Here you go...sesame bagel with chive cream cheese and coffee with cream and two sugars."

"You remembered that about me?" asked Albert.

"It's my job," replied the baker. He sat down with Albert, drinking from his own cup of coffee.

"Can I ask you a question?" Albert inquired. The baker nodded. "Weren't you worried when that man was honking?"

"Worried?" replied the baker. "That was Bud behind you. Retired and always in hurry to go nowhere. No need to worry about him."

"Oh," said Albert.

"I'll tell you something about Bud," said the baker. "He steals my sugar packets and napkins. He thinks I don't notice because I don't say anything."

"I guess he doesn't have much money," suggested Albert.

"He's a retired banker with plenty of money," said the baker. "It's just what he does...that's all. You can't let other people worry you, Albert. Do your own thing and everything will be fine."

Albert nodded and continued to eat his bagel. The baker excused himself for a moment to take care of another customer. Then he came back and sat down with Albert again.

"I'm anxious to hear about the adventures you're planning with that new rig," said the baker, gesturing to where the motor coach was parked.

"Oh," said Albert. "I'm writing the manual for it. It's a new model."

"And you're the first to try out it out?" said the baker. "That's great, Albert. Are you taking a trip in it?"

"I drove around the neighborhood the other day," said Albert. "There was an incident…with a squirrel."

The baker laughed. "Any place else?"

Albert thought for a moment. "Well, I was thinking of taking a trip to some of the national parks."

"That sounds like a great idea," said the baker.

Albert smiled. "Yes," he said. "The manufacturer wants me to really experience the motor coach. To make sure the manual is practical and authentic."

"Makes sense," said the baker.

"It's a lot to handle, though" admitted Albert. "I've never worked on a project this large before."

"I'm sure you can handle it," said the baker. "You've written manuals for years. Didn't you tell me you wrote the manual for my expresso machine?"

"I did," said Albert.

"I couldn't have made heads or tails of that machine without that book," said the baker.

"Thank you," said Albert. "I've never written about anything like the Venture before, though."

"I didn't know anything about baking before I opened this bakery," said the baker. "I was working in an office."

"I didn't know that," replied Albert. "How did you do it?"

"I learned, Albert," explained the baker. "I tried things and I learned. And I made lots of mistakes. I had my share of squirrel incidents."

This made Albert feel a bit better about things.

"When are you leaving for the trip?" asked the baker.

Albert thought about this. "Soon," he said. "I should be leaving soon."

14

"That seems like a lot of clothes, Albert," observed the wallet. "How long is this trip going to be?"

Albert considered this. "I guess I'm not sure," he said. He went to his top drawer and pulled out several more pairs of socks. "I want to be prepared."

"I guess I can't argue with that," said the wallet. "But you know you can't visit all of those places the travel agent showed you. It would take months."

"I know that," said Albert. "The Venture holds plenty of things." He took out a few more shirts and stacked them neatly on the bed.

"You're really going, then?" said the wallet.

"He's going," replied to the cell phone.

"What if you want a bagel…or anything else you're used to having?" asked the wallet.

"I'm fairly sure there are bakeries outside of this town," said the car keys. "And anything else Albert might need."

"I didn't see any bakeries marked on the routes," said the wallet.

"I can find them," said the cell phone. "And the motor coach has a navigation system."

Albert nodded and continued to pack. He carefully lined up all the clothes on his bed before taking out his suitcases. Then he began packing each stack of clothes.

"You haven't learned to use the stove or oven in the motor coach yet," said the wallet. "Maybe you should do that before leaving on the trip."

"That would be prudent," said the reading glasses.

"Yes," said the wallet. "You could leave next week."

"It's a stove," protested the keys. "It works the same as the one here in the house."

"Albert doesn't know that for sure," said the wallet, sounding very skeptical.

"It's dials and nobs," said the keys.

"And there's always take out," added the cell phone. "Or he could ask another camper for help."

"I believe I can figure it out," said Albert.

"Don't say I didn't warn you," said the wallet.

"He can never say that," said the keys.

Albert finished up packing his clothes and gathered incidental items such as his extra toothbrush. He closed the suitcases and took them downstairs. Albert loaded the suitcases into the motor coach.

"What about pots and pans, Albert," suggested the reading glasses.

"That's right," agreed Albert. "I'll need lots of things like that. Albert went around the house picking up essentials such as pots, pans, plates and other items.

He grabbed the clock radio. "I suppose it's back to that infernal machine," said the clock. "You have a habit of ignoring my alarm in there."

Albert continued to roam around the house snatching up things he might need – a small vacuum cleaner, a bottle of dish soap. The motor coach began to fill up quickly.

"See how many things you need, Albert?" pointed out the wallet. "Wouldn't it be easier to just stay here and write the manual?"

Albert surveyed the items he'd brought out to the motor coach. There was still several others he'd thought about and wanted to fetch from the house. He considered the wallet's suggestion. Then he looked out the front windows of the motor coach.

"It might be easier," he said. "But it wouldn't be the same."

15

Albert decided to take one last walk on the nature paths by his home before leaving for his trip. He went on a weekday so he had the walk mainly to himself. He was on his second pass when he noticed an unusually large gathering of ants off to one side. Albert bent down to take a closer look.

Usually the ants stayed on a specific route, one following the other. They moved with purpose and carried bits of leaves or twigs and little grains of sand. However, this time they seemed to be going around in circles, unsure about their way or destination.

Rather than traveling in a straight line, they were bunched into a large clump, some of them even walking over top of each other. Every so often an ant would pause to put its head up, swatting the air with its front legs and antennas. Then it would shake its head and continue walking.

Albert tried to find a reason for their odd behavior. He looked for beetles and other larger insects that might be targeting them. They might be running around scared, unsure of how to get away. Albert didn't see anything that would cause such panic.

Albert considered the idea they had stumbled across a rival group and were trying to guard their territory. He looked more closely at the clump of ants and studied several of them. Albert was by no means an expert on insects, but these ants certainly all looked the same.

Albert stood up and scratched his head. There seemed to be no explanation for their odd behavior. The ants had simply gone off course or become confused in some way. He wondered about their fate if they continued this way. Would they wander aimlessly until they starved and died?

He looked back down again and discovered the group of ants had gotten smaller. "Are they dying that quickly?" He wondered aloud.

Then he noticed a small line of ants filing out from one side of the larger group. They were heading in a direction away from the path and seemed to have some destination in mind. As Albert watched, the clump of ants grew smaller and smaller until they all left via the new line. They disappeared into the thicker, taller plants of the meadow.

Albert smiled and finished up his second and third pass along the path. Even though he was getting hungry he decided to walk the path a fourth time. Then he returned to the car. He turned back for a final look. Albert smiled.

"There are ants on every path," he said.

16

Albert turned his head right and then left, checking for traffic. The street was quiet. "Are you sure you remembered everything?" asked the wallet.

"He's checked everything at least twice," said the car keys.

This was true. Albert had double and triple checked everything. He had reviewed everything he packed from clothes to household items to supplies. He'd gone over every lock in the house several times including the doors and windows. He tried every system on the motor coach to ensure it worked – even the lights he'd checked a couple days before. He'd gone over the routes the travel agent gave him several times and decided on his first destination.

"I'm ready to leave," Albert concluded. Seeing no other cars on the street, he pulled out heading in the direction of the interstate.

"Finally on the road," said the keys.

"Yes," agreed the cell phone.

"Are you watching the mirrors, Albert?" asked the wallet. "You have to keep watching you know."

"I'm looking at the mirrors," said Albert. He maintained a regular pattern of checking each mirror.

"What about your blind spot?" asked the wallet. "Is there anyone in your blind spot?"

"You can't see someone in your blind spot," said the keys. "That's why they call it the blind spot. Otherwise they'd call it the see spot."

"Then how do you avoid hitting things in it?" asked the reading glasses.

"I think it's the job of those people to avoid hitting you," replied the keys.

"How is that supposed to work?" asked the wallet.

"I think they're supposed to stay out of your blind spot," suggested the cell phone.

"That's all well and good," said the wallet, "except how would they know if they're in our blind spot."

"What if we're in someone else's blind spot?" asked the reading glasses.

"Excellent point," replied the wallet. "Albert, are you keeping out of everyone's blind spot?"

Albert looked at the other vehicles around him. He wasn't sure if he was in someone's blind spot or not. "I'm not sure where the blind spots are," he said.

"That guy's in a convertible," said the cell phone. "He probably doesn't even have any blind spots."

"What about that pick up truck with all the furniture tied in the back?" asked the wallet. "The whole thing is one big blind spot."

Albert became very confused. The issue of blind spots suddenly seemed extremely complicated. He thought about the clump of ants again. Suppose they had been caught up in a blind spot. He looked in all the mirrors again. He tapped a button on the navigation display that switched the screen to a rear view camera.

Then he remembered. "The mirrors," he said. "If I can see their mirrors then I'm not in their blind spot. If they can see my mirrors they're not in my blind spot."

"That's right," agreed the keys. "Good thinking Albert."

"All of which brings us back to the same question," said the wallet. "What if someone is in your blind spot?"

"I need to keep them out of my blind spot," replied Albert. As if to test the theory, Albert noticed a small sports car was slipping out of his view. He slowed down to allow it to pass and come back into view.

Albert flipped the screen back to the route. He was almost to the interstate. "In one mile, bear right," announced the navigation system. At the ramp, he bore right as instructed and the motor coach glided up the entrance to the highway. The wide, multi-lane road came into view as he reached the top.

The interstate was crowded and everyone seemed to be in a hurry. Cars and trucks wizzed by him as he approached the merge point. Albert became more and more nervous the closer he got to the point where the lanes came together. He sped up, then thought better of it and slowed back down.

"Albert, this is called the acceleration lane for a reason," said the keys.

Albert sped up again. Then he spotted a car approaching from the left and slowed back down. "Maybe I should pull to the shoulder," he said and flipped on the right turn signal.

"Good idea," said the wallet.

"If you pull over," warned the keys, "you'll never be able to get back into this traffic."

Albert turned off the turn signal and considered both options. "Only you can decide," said the deep voice.

Albert's time was up – he had reached the end of the merge lane. He took a deep breath and guided the motor coach over to the left. There were several honks from behind and a van darted around him. However, he was now on the interstate.

PART 3

1

Albert pressed the button to lower the driver's side window and stuck out his hand. He rolled his fingers up and down as the wind blew past them. He couldn't help but smile. Albert brought his hand back inside and pressed the button to roll up the window. He enjoyed the breeze but he found the noise too distracting.

Albert's struggle to get on the interstate was now a distant memory. He was navigating the motor coach down the center lane, watching the world wiz by him through the large windows at the front of the vehicle.

Every fifteen minutes, Albert checked each of the side mirrors and reviewed the vehicle's panels and gauges. The oil pressure looked good, the temperature was in the green and he had plenty of fuel. "The Venture features two fuel tanks to keep you on the road longer," he'd written a couple of days ago.

The last item he checked during this routine was the navigation display. Albert enjoyed glancing at his progress along the marked path. However, he noticed something that concerned him. Below the map the system showed his approximate arrival time.

"It'll be past sunset before I arrive," Albert observed. "I'll have to back into the campsite in the dark."

"Of course you will," replied the keys. At that moment two other vehicles roared past him on either side of the motor coach. Albert watched them go by and get smaller and smaller.

"This is the interstate," said the keys. "You're driving at the half the speed limit in the center lane."

"I'm operating at a safe speed," said Albert.

"This would be safe speed for a funeral procession," replied the keys.

"Ignore that," said the wallet. "You need to stay safe and comfortable."

" I won't be very comfortable parking at night," said Albert. The wallet didn't seem to have an answer for that particular problem.

"Then we'd better pick up the pace," said the keys. Other vehicles continued to roar past Albert on both sides. Some blew the horn as they went past.

Albert weighed his options. He was nervous about going faster but he wanted to arrive at the campsite before dark. "Maybe I could pull over to the side of the road and stay there for the night."

"That would be a failure, Albert," said the keys. "You don't want to quit now."

Albert nodded. He didn't want to quit now. Sleeping in the motor coach by the side of the road didn't seem much different than sleeping while parked in the driveway.

"At least you wouldn't have to worry about the neighbor's car alarm," the wallet pointed out.

He decided he didn't have much of a choice and pressed down harder on the gas. The motor coach increased in speed. Albert gripped the wheel tighter and began to check the mirrors more frequently. He looked down at the navigation display and was reassured to find the time estimate was growing progressively smaller.

"Good Albert," said the reading glasses from their position in one of the unused cup holders. "A bit faster and you'll get there shortly before dark."

Albert was pleased with this idea. He smiled a bit and pressed on the gas a little more until and watched as the time estimate dropped again.

"This feels too fast," cautioned the wallet.

"Pipe down," said keys.

Albert gripped the wheel and smiled a bit wider. The motor coach actually seemed easier to handle at the faster speed. After a few more miles, he even rolled the window down again. Taking a firm hold on the wheel with one hand he placed the other back out the window. He rolled it in the wind as he continued down the road.

2

Albert brought the motor coach to a stop in front of the campground's registration office. There was a note pinned to the door, addressed to him.

"Albert: Welcome to Pine Lake. Had to fix a broken water hookup. You're in Site 25. Make yourself at home and we'll settle up in the morning."

Albert found this a little unsettling, but a glance at the sky showed him he had at least forty-five minutes of daylight left. He returned to the motor coach and slowly made his way to a large fork in the road. He followed the sign for sites twenty through thirty and reached Site 25 a few moments later.

He pulled past the site and made an attempt to back into it. "You're cutting the wheel too much," said the wallet as the rear of the vehicle swung towards a tree."

"You're not cutting it enough," disagreed the keys.

"I think you're not going fast enough," added the cell phone.

"No, no," said the reading glasses. "He's going too fast."

Albert looked from mirror to mirror to rear view camera and back to the mirrors again. He jerked the wheel back and forth in an attempt to center the back of the motor coach. It was clear he was not going to make it into the site on this attempt so he pulled out of the site and back onto the road.

"You're already at an angle," said the wallet.

Albert pulled backward and forward in an attempt to straighten the motor coach in the road. "You're making it worse," said the keys. "You should try backing in again."

"Or we could ask for help," suggested the cell phone. Albert scanned the area. All of the other campers were either inside their recreational vehicles or engrossed in conversation around a campfire.

"I don't want to be a bother," said Albert.

He made several more attempts to back into the site. With each try he seemed to have less and less room. "Albert," said the keys, "try steering from the bottom of the wheel."

"That's not right," said the cell phone. "Turn the opposite of the direction you want the back of the vehicle to swing."

"That's only if you're towing," said the reading glasses. "In this case you want turn the way you want to go."

The more Albert tried, the more confused he became and the more daylight he lost.

"What about those people around that fire across the way?" asked the cell phone.

Albert looked over at the group. They were all laughing. He was sure he saw one of them look over their shoulder at him. "I don't think that's a good idea," he said.

Albert got out of the motor coach and retrieved a tape measure from a tool box on the outside of the vehicle. He began measuring the site from various angles and distances. Albert went back inside to scribble notes and drawings. He drew arcs and calculated angles.

"How is all of this geometry going to help?" asked the keys.

"This is actually trigonometry," corrected the wallet.

"Then how is all of this trigonometry going to help?" asked the keys. "Maybe you should just close your eyes and go for it," suggested the keys.

Albert stared at his notes and drawings, comparing them to his view of the site in the mirrors and rear view camera. Eventually he crumpled up the papers and got back out of the motor coach. This time he lined up sticks in the shape of arrows throughout the site.

Albert got behind the wheel once again and made another attempt. He was about a quarter of the way into the site before he heard the crunching of sticks as he road over several of his arrows. This was immediately followed by a steady beep...beep...beep coming from the navigational display.

"The Venture is equipped with a proximity alarm designed to help you avoid hazards," recited Albert. He stopped the vehicle just before hitting a tree. He put his hands on either side of his head and rested his forehead against the steering wheel.

Albert sat like that for several minutes. The woods were fairly quiet, other than the mechanics of the engine and the occasional loud voice or burst of laughter from around the nearby campfires. He looked up to discover that the light was nearly gone, especially here in within the woods of the campground.

Albert pulled out of the site and travelled down the road. He discovered it was a loop that brought him right back to the same campsite. This time he did not pass it but simply turned the wheel and pulled straight into it. "There," he announced. "I was able to park before losing the daylight."

"Barely," said the wallet. "And you pulled in front first."

Albert didn't care. He was relieved to have the Venture in the site. He was also exhausted and ready to go to bed. "I don't know why anyone backs in at all," Albert observed.

He got up from the driver's seat and walked back to the short couch that served as the motor coach's living room. It was now very dark so Albert reached out and flipped on one of the light switches. A red light on the panel indicated he was using the battery, reminding him to hook up the electric and water lines.

Albert grabbed a flash light and went back outside yet again. He located the storage bins with the electric chord and hose and attached them to the hook ups on the motor coach. Then he began scanning the edge of the site with the flashlight. He knew from his research that somewhere there would be a post with the site's electric and water sources.

After several moments of searching, he started to wonder if the site even had these features. Then a thought occurred to Albert and he walked to the other side of the campsite. He found the electric and water sources almost immediately. Albert sighed and walked back to the other side of the motor coach to retrieve the electric cord.

He carried the cord across the front of the vehicle and started down the other side. Albert got about four feet before the cord jerked backward pulling him with it. It was clearly too short to go completely around the vehicle. Albert suddenly understood the reason most people backed into the site.

3

Albert was drinking his morning coffee when he spotted someone through the window of the motor coach. He put down his cup and stepped outside. An older man in a shirt embroidered with the campground logo was standing at the edge of the site. The man nodded to Albert and walked over to get a closer look at the way Albert had hooked up the electric and water by cracking a window on each side and running the cord and hose through it.

"Interesting approach," said the man. "You must be Albert. My name's Joe. I left you the note on the door."

"Hello," said Albert. "I had some trouble backing in."

"I've been the caretaker here for over twenty years," the man replied. "I can't say that's the strangest thing I've ever seen."

Albert had no immediate reply. He reached into his pocket and pulled out the old watch. He'd been carrying it with him since he left the house. "Have you seen a watch like this before?" he asked.

The caretaker looked at watch. "It's a nice watch," he said. "Interesting inscription."

"Have you seen anything like it?" asked Albert.

"Can't say I have," said the caretaker. He handed Albert a pamphlet. "Here are maps of the campground and the surrounding park."

"Thank you," replied Albert.

The caretaker nodded and reached into his pocket. He pulled out three ribbons, two yellow and one pink. "When you don't have a spotter," he said, "tie the two yellows at the back of the site to mark your sides. Put the pink ribbon in between. Keep the sides of the coach inside those yellows and try to get the pink in the center."

"Spotter?" asked Albert.

"Someone to guide you in," said the caretaker. "Why don't you disconnect those hook ups and we'll give it a try."

Albert nodded and unplugged the electric and water. The caretaker showed him places to hang the ribbons and guided him into the site. He also taught him standard hand signals.

"Good," he said after Albert had managed to back the vehicle into the site. "Now try again with just your mirrors and the ribbons. It's good to have a spotter but it doesn't always work out that way."

Albert pulled the motor coach out of the site and backed into it again using the caretaker's strategy. It took a few additional tries, but he managed to get the motor coach into the site on his own.

"There you go," said the caretaker.

"Thank you," said Albert.

"Don't mention it," said the caretaker. "Keep in mind no one knows the right way to do things on the first try. The more you do it, the better you'll get."

Albert nodded.

"I'm usually in the office if I'm not out fixing something," said the caretaker. "Enjoy your stay."

After the caretaker left, Albert decided that a bicycle ride might be a good way to get to know his new surroundings. He walked to the back of the motor coach and began removing the straps holding the bicycle on the rack.

"I thought you forgot about me," said the bicycle. "I've been hanging here for days."

"It's been three days," said Albert.

"Exactly," said the bicycle. "I have bugs stuck to my frame."

"There's a hose," said Albert. "I'll rinse you off before we go."

"How delightful," replied the bicycle.

Albert retrieved the bicycle from the rack and set it gingerly on the ground. He retrieved the hose and washed down the frame. Then he wiped the seat and the rims of the tires.

"How is that?" asked Albert.

"Better I suppose," said the bicycle. "I guess the roads here are made of dirt."

"They are," replied Albert. "But they're very compact. Almost as good as the streets at home."

"The streets at home aren't all that good," replied the bicycle.

Albert got onto the bike and headed out onto the road. He made his way through the campground, being careful to avoid any ruts or bumps. Most of the campers waved as he passed by them. Albert waved back.

"People here are certainly friendly," said the bicycle. "No one waves to us at home."

"I know," Albert agreed. A couple passed them on the other side of the road, also riding bicycles. Albert exchanged "hello's" with them.

"On your left," came a voice behind him. Albert turned around as a young man biked past him. "Great day for a ride," the man called over his shoulder.

"Yes," said Albert.

"Enjoy it," said the man before he went out of sight around a curve.

"They also don't wear those funny outfits," said Albert.

"What outfits?" asked the bicycle.

"You know," said Albert, "the bicycle outfits. The tight pants, the shirts, the odd-shaped helmets."

"Those are designed to cut down on wind resistance," explained the bicycle.

"You mean around the neighborhood?" asked Albert.

"You really know little about bicycles Albert," said the bicycle.

"I suppose so," said Albert. They passed another couple riding bikes. "Hello," said Albert.

"Hello," they cheerily answered back. They were wearing the bicycle outfits.

"Are those outfits really necessary?" asked Albert.

"I suppose not," said the bicycle. "Unless you're in some kind of competition."

"The salesman tried to get me to buy a couple of those outfits," said Albert.

"That's true," said the bicycle.

"I don't think I'd look very good in one of those outfits," said Albert.

"I don't suppose you would," said the bicycle. "I don't suppose anyone really does.'

4

Albert compared his map with the posted trail guide at the edge of the park. He decided to take the blue trail. The guide indicated it was fairly level, and although it ran about a mile it did not stray far from the park entrance. The path twisted it's way along the edge before returning to its starting point.

Albert started down the blue trail. His original intention was to walk similar to the way he did near home – observing one side of the path on each pass. However, he quickly found himself overwhelmed with the newness of everything and couldn't help from darting his eyes back and forth.

He saw trees, plants and insects he'd never observed before. This path wound its way through tall pines skirted by knee high ferns and mosses. Occasionally a beetle would scurry its way along the path. Albert didn't see any ants, although he was sure there had to be some.

About halfway down the path Albert came across a bench fashioned from pine wood logs. He decided to sit down and enjoy the quiet for awhile – except that Albert discovered it wasn't all that quiet. These woods were noisy.

As Albert sat still on the bench he could hear the rustle of wind through the trees, the chirping of the birds and the bending of branches as animals made their way around. If the path near his home was a rural small town, these woods were a major city.

"It's like some sort of ecological metropolis," Albert said out loud to no one in particular. Still, he did find it peaceful in its on way. It was certainly better than a car horn or lawn mower.

And it was interesting. Albert found the woods similar to the mechanical objects he'd written about, such as clocks and appliances. The forest was like a machine unto itself that bustled about in its own organic way.

He came to the conclusion that he hadn't seen any ants because they were probably toiling away in the high rise of a tree or factory of a fallen long. The ants were too small to be seen in such an overwhelming collection of flora and fauna.

They were lost among the details here. Albert imagined them moving along their single file paths carrying around leaves and other bits. They were surrounded by a hundred other plants and animals doing other things – probably more important things, Albert reasoned.

Albert got up from the bench and continued along the path. He eventually arrived at a small stream. The introduction of water added yet another new dimension to Albert's walk. Now he was able to observe insects skimming along the surface, fish swimming above the rocks and the occasional salamander crawling along the banks.

"This would be the port of call," Albert observed.

He spent a long time at the stream and did something he'd never done before – Albert left the established path. He walked up and down the banks of the stream to get a better look. He followed a fish as it chased insects on top of the water and then watched a bird eyeing the fish from a nearby tree.

After awhile Albert noticed the sun was no longer in the middle of the sky. It was now sitting halfway above the horizon. He decided it was time to head back to the campsite and do some writing before dinner and eventually bed.

5

Albert couldn't remember the last time he was this tired. He'd spent the better part of the day on the trail and then written about the motor coach for most of the late afternoon and evening. His only break was for a quick dinner of macaroni and cheese cooked on the stove. Albert hadn't gotten around to learning much about the Venture's appliances yet.

He laid down on the bed in the back room of the motor coach and stared up at the plastic window placed in the ceiling. Hinges and a small crank allowed it to double as a vent to let in fresh air on mild nights. Even though trees hung over the campsite, Albert could still make out a number of stars through the branches. It was more stars than he could see at home and they all seemed brighter.

As he laid there, Albert listened for the sounds of the woods. Unlike his time on the trail he heard almost nothing. There was only the low steady chirping of crickets, reminding Albert of a white noise machine he had once written about.

"The white noise machine didn't sound as good," concluded Albert.

"The white noise machine?" asked the clock on the mantle. "You didn't bring that along, did you Albert?"

"It was annoying," said the keys.

"I think we're all in agreement about that," said the reading glasses.

Albert closed his eyes but was surprised to find that he did not fall asleep. "I know I'm tired," he said.

"Don't tell me you miss the car alarm," said the wallet. "Or perhaps the garbage truck that comes at six in the morning."

"I don't miss any of the sounds from home," said Albert. "But it is very quiet here at night."

"That's not necessarily a bad thing," said the reading glasses.

"It is different," said Albert. He laid there trying to decide whether different meant better or worse. "Maybe that just means different," he decided.

"Only you can decide," said the deep voice.

"I always sleep well at home," said Albert.

"This is only your second night in the motor coach," pointed out the keys.

"Third night," corrected the wallet.

"I'm not counting the night parked in the drive way," clarified the keys.

"It doesn't matter either way, since you didn't set the alarm," mourned the clock.

"You don't set alarms on vacation," explained the cell phone.

"This is not vacation," the wallet pointed out. "This is technically a business trip."

"Can't it be both?" asked the reading glasses.

"I'm not even going to respond to that," said the wallet.

"Because you have no response," said the cell phone.

Albert continued to stare at the skylight and listen to the crickets. "Definitely better than the car alarm," he concluded.

"You might as well admit you're having fun, Albert," said the cell phone.

"Yes, Albert," said the wallet. "Admit you're having fun." The request seemed much harsher.

"I am having fun," said Albert.

"I knew it," said the wallet and the cell phone together. They would have been in harmony had their tones not been so different.

"At least the two of you agree," said the reading glasses.

"Don't encourage them," said the keys.

Albert replayed the events of the day in his mind. He had backed the motor coach into the site, taken a long hike and written several pages. He closed his eyes again and listened to the crickets. Albert was not at home but he did manage to fall asleep.

6

"How much wood do you need?" asked the wallet. "This is not a pep rally. You don't need a bonfire to roast a couple of hot dogs."

"I need more smaller sticks for kindling," Albert explained.

"You need to use the stove," said the wallet. "Hot dogs over a fire…the idea. You're not twelve years old anymore."

"You really are no fun at all," said the cell phone.

"It's a cheap dinner," said the keys. "Isn't that one of your core values?"

"If it were up to you," replied the wallet, "Albert would never have any money."

Albert began building the base of his fire. He crumpled newspaper in the center and surrounded that with the small sticks. Then he carefully placed larger pieces of wood against the tent-like structure. Albert set each piece carefully. He didn't want to knock down the rest of the sticks and paper.

Albert stood back to admire his work. "That should do it," he said. He picked up a piece of paper and twisted it into a long tube. He struck a match and held it under the paper tube until the end caught fire. Albert set the burning wad of paper down at the base of the pile and it wasn't long before the paper in the middle of the pile began to burn, followed by the sticks.

Albert became worried as the pile began to collapse, until he realized it did not matter. The kindling and even the large sticks had already caught fire. With the flames becoming higher and steadier, Albert placed a large log in the middle. He watched to make sure it caught fire. Then he placed another log on top of it. Not long afterward, a glowing pile of coals began to form at the base of the fire.

"I think you're ready to cook Albert," said the reading glasses.

"All of your clothes are going to smell like smoke," said the wallet.

Albert smelled his sleeve. It did smell like smoke but he didn't mind. He was proud of the fire and excited to cook on it. He walked over to a cooler and took out a package of hot dogs. Albert placed two hot dogs on a metal skewer and held them over the fire, close to the coals around the main logs.

He propped the skewer on some rocks and went to retrieve a tray with buns and condiments. Albert set this down near the fire and turned over the hot dogs.

"Processed meat on a metal stick," observed the wallet. "Not exactly the most healthy dinner."

"Classic camp food," declared the cell phone.

"I suppose you're having s'mores after this?" asked the wallet.

"As a matter of fact," Albert began. His thought was interrupted as one of the hot dogs caught on fire. He grabbed the skewer from the rocks, tilting one of the hot dogs even further into the fire. It was still burning when he pulled it out. Albert began to blow on it, continuing until he was out of breath. The hot dog was still smoking when placed it on a bun.

"Mustard fixes everything," suggested the car keys.

"Please tell me you're not going to eat that," said the wallet.

Albert applied a generous amount of mustard to the hot dog and took a bite. "A bit smoky," he said. "But not too bad." He went on the eat three more hot dogs, making sure to catch each one on fire first.

"I don't even know who you are anymore," said the wallet.

By the time Albert was finished eating, the fire had burnt most of the way down, leaving only hot glowing coals.

"Perfect for s'more," suggested the cell phone.

Albert already felt full but was considering the idea until a flicker caught the corner of his eye. He went over to investigate. He initially found nothing and was about to turn back to the fire when a small flame appeared in front of him.

Drawing a shallow breath, Albert rushed over to grab a shovel leaning against the motor coach. He ran back over to the small flame and banged on it with the shovel until it disappeared. Breathing a sigh of relief, he started to walk away when another flicker caught his attention. Albert rushed over to discover another flame.

He was stamping out the second flame when two others popped up several feet away. Albert put these out with the shovel, only to discover yet another. He put this one out as well. Afterward, he stood scanning the campsite. The danger appeared to over so he returned the shovel to its resting place against the motor coach.

As the handle touched the side of the coach, two new fires appeared nearby. Albert ran over and put both of these out, only to spot one more. This continued for about an hour, with Albert stomping out several more small fires. Exhausted, he sat next to the original fire. The number of coals had grown smaller but the ones in the center still glowed hot.

"What is going on?" he wondered.

"Ghost fires?" suggested the cell phone.

"Spontaneous combustion?" added the reading glasses.

"I'm sure it's something more logical than that," said the wallet.

"Did you drop any coals anywhere?" asked the car keys. "Or bits of burning hot dog?"

Albert got up and looked around the campsite. While making his rounds he had to put out two more small fires. They seemed to appear from nowhere. There were no burning coals or even blackened bits of hot dog.

Frustrated, Albert went back to the original fire and stomped it with the shovel until no lit coals remained. He turned the dirt over several times. "I think I will forgo the s'mores for this evening," he announced.

Albert looked around the site for several minutes. No other fires appeared. "It's like they were little satellite fires," he said.

"Maybe the embers were blowing around," said the keys.

"At least that's plausible," said the wallet.

Albert considered this idea but wasn't convinced. He looked down into the remains of the original fire, turning the ashes over with the shovel. Curious, he dug down a bit and discovered a couple of places where the fire seemed to have burned into the ground.

"Roots," he realized. "I should have cleared the roots." He turned the ashes and dirt around for awhile, just to be sure. Then he gathered the remains of his dinner and returned to the motor coach.

Back inside Albert thought for few moments. He placed a marshmallow on the end of one of the metal skewers. Then Albert turned on the stove and held the marshmallow over it. He did allow it to catch on fire, but quickly blew it out and turned off the stove. Albert placed the still warm marshmallow and a piece of chocolate between two graham crackers. He smiled as he took a bite.

7

Albert returned from his daily nature walk feeling unsettled. He poured himself a glass of juice and sat down at the table in the motor coach. While snacking on some crackers he looked through the trail guides. Over the past few days Albert had taken every route, some several times. Something was odd about today's walk, though.

Reflecting on his routine, Albert couldn't think of anything that had gone differently. He'd taken a path he'd enjoyed many times. He saw the same plants and trees, even some of the same animals. It hadn't taken any more or less time than the previous days. The weather was even similar.

Albert realized that was the problem. The trails here had become no different than the one at home. He knew every turn, rise and dip. While that was fine for his path near home, it somehow seemed wrong for these trails.

"What is the point if I already know the trail?" he said.

"I thought that was the point," said the reading glasses.

"I used to think it was the point," replied Albert. "Now I'm not so sure."

"Time to move on," said the car keys.

"Back home?" asked the wallet.

Albert looked through the brochures he'd gotten from the travel agent. "The next park looks even bigger," said Albert.

"If you turn back now," suggested the wallet, "you could finish the manual at home and turn it in well ahead of schedule."

Albert looked out the window of the motor coach. "I don't think I could finish this manual at home," he said. Albert spent the rest of the day packing things up and making sure loose items were secured. He would leave for the next destination in the morning.

For the first time in several days he set the alarm clock so he could get an early start in the morning. He had a longer distance to go for the next destination and he needed to fill the motor coach with fuel.

Albert got a good night's sleep. Early the next morning he ate a quick breakfast and disconnected the electric and water from the Venture. He drove back to the office to settle his bill.

"Here's your total for the site," said the caretaker handing him a receipt. "And I suppose you'll need to dump your tank before you get back on the road."

"Dump the tank?" asked Albert.

"Yes," said the caretaker. "You know...your unmentionables. Fee is fifty-five dollars, valve is over there. You can pull straight around."

Albert considered for a moment. He knew about the tank and it's purpose and he had certainly used the facilities in the motor coach. However, he hadn't given much thought to the actual task of dumping the tank.

"This is exactly the reason you need to head for home immediately," said the wallet.

"I bet it's like a bandaid," said the keys. "Best to just rip it off."

"Slow and steady wins the race, Albert," said the reading glasses.

"Ask for help," suggested the cell phone.

"I take it this is your first time," said the caretaker. "How about I walk you through it."

Albert nodded. "Thank you," he said.

Albert looked at his chapped hands. "That's probably because you washed them so many times," said the car keys.

"And now you are well off schedule," said the wallet. "You'll never make it to your next destination today or possibly even tomorrow."

Albert looked at his hands again and sighed. He realized he'd probably have to wash again after pumping the gas. A sign indicated there was a station off the next exit, so Albert decided to get the task out of the way.

He pulled the motor coach into the station and up to one of the pumps. Albert got out and began to look for the gas cap. "You should have checked this back at the campground," pointed out the wallet.

"I was pre-occupied there," said Albert. He had reached the rear of the Venture without finding the gas cap. "It's on the other side," he realized.

"Typical example of poor planning," said the wallet.

Albert sighed and walked over to the other side of the vehicle. He could see the square outline of the cover. He also hadn't thought to pull the release in the cab. Albert looked at the width of the motor coach and then back at the hose on the pump.

"Are you going to run the hose through the windows?" asked the reading glasses.

"I'll turn the motor coach around," said Albert. He got back inside the vehicle and pulled away from the pump. The area was tighter than he anticipated, so Albert pulled completely out of the gas station and into another one across the street. This time he pulled onto the correct side of the pump.

"The gas is three cents more expensive at this station," said the wallet.

"Does it really matter?" asked the car keys.

"No," replied the wallet. "Albert can just throw money away."

"It is only about thirty cents difference overall," explained the reading glasses.

"Of course," said the wallet sarcastically. "Its only money. Albert, why don't you throw a couple of dollars in that trash bin while you're here. It doesn't matter."

Albert sighed even louder and went about filling the motor coach with gas. As he was waiting for the pump to finish, another motor coach pulled next to him. A jovial looking man in a ripped baseball cap immediately jumped out.

"Well hey there," he said as he started operating the pump on his side.

Albert wasn't sure if this was a greeting or the start of a question. He decided to give a slight nod.

"Nice rig you've got there," continued the man.

Once again, Albert was not sure of the man's meaning. This must have shown on his face because the man gestured towards the motor coach.

"Thank you," said Albert.

"Great day to be on the road," continued the man. He stood at pump holding the nozzle rather than using the clip to hold it open.

Albert looked up at the sky. It was getting very overcast and a storm seemed inevitable. He felt it was best to nod nonetheless.

The man chuckled. "I know what you're thinking," he said gesturing towards the clouds. "Any day on the road is a good one...rain or shine."

"Who are you talking to, Harvey?" came a woman's voice from the other side.

"Fellow camper," replied Harvey.

The woman emerged. She had three small dogs on leashes. "Oh," she said. "I'm taking the children to the facilities." She gestured to a sticker on the camper that read 'my kids have paws.' One of the dogs began to relieve itself on the gas pump. "You know better than that," she said to the dog, but she didn't stop it.

"You should take them over to the bushes," said Harvey shaking his head and rolling his eyes.

Albert's pump made a clicking sound to indicate it was finished. He put the pump back and replaced the gas cap.

"You got two tanks on that rig?" asked Harvey.

"Yes," replied Albert. He hastily pressed the button for no receipt and headed back to the door of the motor coach.

"Maybe we'll see you up the road," Harvey called out as Albert got back into the coach. Albert looked back and nodded. He started the Venture and pulled out the station.

"That was rather unsociable of you Albert," said the cell phone.

"They were a little strange," said the car keys.

"Quirky," said the cell phone. "This trip is an opportunity to meet interesting people."

"I don't believe Albert is obligated to talk to random people at gas pumps simply because they have recreational vehicles," said the wallet.

"They seemed friendly enough," said the reading glasses.

"Until they grind you up for kibble to feed the dogs," said the wallet.

"It's starting to rain," said Albert. "I'd better find somewhere to park for the night."

"Look for someplace that doesn't allow pets," suggested the wallet.

9

Albert put down the driver's side window and placed his hand outside to feel the wind. The weather had cleared up and he was making good time towards the next park. He enjoyed watching the scenery roll by the motor coach…and not just the greenery.

Albert liked reading the billboards, looking at passing buildings and even the other vehicles on the road. He appreciated the newness of it all. Even a billboard about a soft drink or chewing gum was interesting because it was usually one he'd never seen before.

"It's the bubbliest," claimed one the sign.

"Fewest calories," boasted another.

"Longest chewing satisfaction," proclaimed another.

"Dinosaurs," the latest billboard announced.

"Dinosaurs," Albert repeated.

Several other billboards shouted their messages as they passed. "Best food." "Cleanest rooms." "Closest shave."

And there it was again…"Dinosaurs…live and uncaged."

"Hmmm," wondered Albert.

"Fast service." "The number one fuel." "Open 24 hours."

Yet again…"Dinosaurs. Next exit. Don't miss it."

"Dinosaurs," said Albert. "That could be interesting."

"You just got back on schedule," said the wallet. "If that place had live dinosaurs I think you would have seen it on the news."

"It sounds fun," said the cell phone. "You should stop, Albert."

"It is on the way," said the reading glasses.

"Did the travel agent give you a brochure about it?" asked the wallet.

"I don't have a brochure on it," Albert admitted.

"If it was good," said the wallet, "the agent would have mentioned it.

"Dinosaurs! Exit Now!" urged the next billboard.

Albert decided to turn off the exit. He followed the signs and pulled the motor coach into the parking lot. He got out and walked up to the main building, which looked like a large western style lodge. Albert strained to see a shape slightly above the building. He realized it actually looked like the head of a dinosaur.

Albert went into the building and paid admission to the park. He was directed to a door leading out of the back of the building. Once outside, he found himself in a large field with several walkways. The walkways led to full scale representations of dinosaurs. These were not quite like the more modern renderings of the large creatures. They reminded Albert of the ways people imagined dinosaurs when he was growing up.

"This is about what I expected," declared the wallet. "Might as well throw that money out with the extra you paid for gas yesterday."

Albert laughed out loud. They certainly weren't real dinosaurs and they didn't even look the way scientists said they should look. However, Albert couldn't help finding them charming in their own way. "This is what I came here to see," he said.

"Cartoon dinosaur statues?" asked the car keys. "I admit I was on the wrong side of this one."

"I would have rather you talked to the people at the gas station," said the cell phone."

"You came on this trip to write a manual Albert," said the wallet.

"It was an interesting stop," said the reading glasses.

Albert spent the next two hours at the site, exploring the rest of the grounds and taking pictures of the various "exhibits." He even ate lunch at the small on-site restaurant inside the main building. In addition to the large statues the attraction also featured several terrariums filled with modern reptiles or "living dinosaurs" as they were described on signage.

All and all it was one of his favorite days of the trip so far. He bought a snow globe and a baseball cap from the gift shop before returning to the motor coach. As he left the attraction a familiar billboard declared "Dinosaurs! Thank you and come again soon."

10

It was very late by the time Albert reached his next destination and set up camp. He looked at the parked motor coach and completed hookups with pride. This time he'd done everything in the dark. Afterward he had a cup of tea and flopped into bed.

"I suppose you won't be setting the alarm tonight," said the clock. Albert didn't answer. He was already snoring. That night he dreamt of dinosaurs roaming the woods around him. They were the shape and colors of the campy ones he'd seen at the park. The dinosaurs posed for pictures and allowed people to feed them. The people were feeding them popcorn.

Albert waited in line to buy some popcorn to feed the dinosaurs. The sound of the kernels popping was loud. It seemed to be all around him. Albert was next in line. The person in front of him finished. Albert stepped forward but found himself lying in his bed in the motor coach. However, the sound of popcorn popping was still all around him. He sat up in bed and looked around.

Most of the sound was coming from the ceiling. The rest was echoing off the walls. Albert leaned over and peeked out of the curtains. A strong rain was falling. It sounded like popcorn as the drops beat on the roof of the motor coach. Albert looked up and watched the drops hitting the plastic skylight above.

He looked at the clock and saw it was just after ten in the morning. "I believe this is the latest you've ever slept," said the clock.

Despite the time of day it was still relatively dark inside the motor coach, so Albert turned on one of the light fixtures hanging by the side of the bed. He got up and went about his morning routine. Albert considered cooking some eggs but decided it was already late so he opted for a bowl of cereal as a quicker option.

"It looks like you're stuck inside today," said the cell phone.

"It's a good day to catch up on some work, Albert," instructed the wallet. "You haven't written in two days."

After breakfast Albert washed his plate and set his portable computer up on the table. "The Venture features a refrigerator that runs on electric or propane," he wrote. "Use the power mode switch from one to the other. Remember to hook up to outside electric service before switching the mode to electric. Check the propane levels before switching to propane."

Albert went on to finish the sections on motor coach's appliances. He decided this was a good amount of writing for the day and put the computer away.

"I believe you're about three-quarters of the way done," said the wallet. "You can probably finish up during your return trip."

Albert ignored the wallet and took out his brochures and maps. His current plan was to spend two or three days here walking the trails and then move onto to another park about half a days drive. A day or so in that park and then onto another. Two days drive after that he'd be at the park with the waterfalls.

"Maybe you should just move on to the next park, Albert," suggested the car keys. "The trails here are likely to be wet anyway."

"He hasn't been here that long," objected the reading glasses. "It isn't a good idea to keep hopping from place to place."

"I agree," said the cell phone. "He hasn't even met anyone here yet, and the people look friendly."

"And what exactly makes a person look friendly?" asked the wallet.

"He doesn't need to talk to someone everywhere he goes," said the keys. "Move on now and you'll get to the waterfalls faster."

Albert considered this for a moment. "You do want to see the waterfalls," said the reading glasses. "The trails looked interesting here too, though."

"Head for home and you eliminate the whole dilemma," said the wallet.

"Or you could lock the wallet in the closet," said car keys.

"I agree," said the cell phone.

"The very idea," stammered the wallet.

"It's been nothing but negative the whole trip," the clock called out from the bedroom. "Even I haven't been that miserable and you're not even using me that often."

The motor coach became very quiet. Even the popcorn sound died out as the rain stopped. "I'm only trying to be the voice of reason," said the wallet.

"This whole project would have gone easier if it wasn't for all your details," said the car keys.

"And you never want to interact with people," said the cell phone. "You mistrust everyone."

Albert looked at the reading glasses. They had been silent since the discussion had begun. "Whatever you think is best," they said at last.

Albert decided he didn't want to talk to the wallet anymore. He put it into the closet as the keys had suggested. Immediately he felt a sense of emptiness and regret. So much so that he almost got the wallet back out.

"Be strong, Albert," urged the keys.

Albert went over to the counter in the galley of the motor coach. He opened one of the drawers. Inside was the old watch. Albert took out the watch and set it by his other things.

11

A couple of hours later the weather had cleared up enough for Albert to walk one of the trails in the park.

The sun was out and the ground was drying quickly. He chose a trail from the guide and started on his way. After only a short time it felt like he was deep in the forest. Albert was surrounded by old growth trees and the ground on either side of the trail was thick with ferns and moss.

Albert took the walk slowly and frequently checked his progress on the trail guide. He had developed a habit of counting steps that allowed him to always have a general idea of his position.

After Albert had walked a couple of hours, he could feel the trail begin to turn back towards the starting point. He'd found that most of the trails in these parks followed a sort of out and back pattern. You spent half time walking away from your starting point and then rest of the time walking back towards it.

He continued to walk for another hour, realizing that he was almost back. The walk had been mostly uneventful. The most interesting aspect had been the water droplets on most of the plants. Albert had never traveled a path this soon after a rain storm. He was amazed at the slow and subtle ways the rain water made its way along the branches, sticks and leaves. Many times the drops would cause a small prism of color as light passed through it.

He was studying one of these small bursts of color when he saw movement out of the corner of his eye. Albert looked up and saw a shadowy figure in the distance. It was only there for a moment. He continued to stare in that direction for a couple of minutes. As soon as he looked away he saw the flash again. This time the shadow grew larger until Albert was able to see it was some type of furry animal.

He was sure it must be some kind of dog until he saw two smaller shapes following behind it. Every few steps the larger animal would pause and wait for the two others. They were getting closer to Albert with each step. A shiver ran through him as he realized he was looking at a bear and two cubs.

He froze where he stood, afraid to even take a breath. Albert had read several trail guides before the trip. They all cautioned against feeding or interacting with bears. And they stressed how the danger increased with a mother bear and her cubs.

Albert continued to stand still, taking only short shallow breaths. He watched as the bears got closer to his position. Eventually the mother bear spotted him, taking a long look at Albert. Albert tried to stay as motionless as possible. The mother bear looked him up and down, then let out a snort. Albert's heart skipped a beat.

"Is this how it ends," he wondered, "mauled by a bear?" A headline flashed across his mind: "Manual writer mauled by bear, instructions not included."

He realized the headline didn't even make sense. "Instructions not included – what did that even mean?" He thought. Then the bear snorted again. She took another look at Albert and gathered her cubs. The trio turned slightly and headed off in another direction. Albert watched them until he could no longer see their shapes in the forest. He remained in the same position long after they had left the area.

Finally he took a deep breath and started walking along the path once again. He no longer noticed water droplets or prisms. He spent the time looking side to side, trying to see as deep into the woods as possible. The bears never returned and Albert reached the end of the trail. He kept walking until he reached the camping area and his site. He didn't totally feel safe until he was back inside the motor coach with the doors locked.

Once he reached safety, however, he couldn't help feeling somewhat exhilarated. Albert had never come that close to a wild animal before – except for the zoo, of course.

"I can't believe I was that close to a bear," he said out loud as he turned the cell phone back on.

"Now that is something you should put in the manual," said the car keys.

"It would make a great campfire story," said the cell phone. "Maybe you should visit your neighbors and tell them about it."

"I'm just glad you're back safe and sound," said the reading glasses.

"The time is six thirty-seven," was the only commentary offered by the old watch.

12

"Well hey there, neighbor. Long time, no see," said a familiar-sounding voice nearby. Albert was getting a can of soup out of one of the outside storage units on the motor coach. He recognized the voice but he couldn't quite place it. Then the owner of the voice stepped out of the trees. It was Harvey, the man he'd met at the gas station. He had one of the small dogs in tow.

"Who are you talking to now, Harvey?" asked his wife, who had the other two dogs with her. "Oh…well doesn't that just beat all?" she said when she saw Albert.

"This is my wife, Edna," said Harvey. "And these are our children: Chocolate, Caramel and Fudge." Harvey gestured towards the dogs. Fudge began sniffing at Albert's leg.

"Now that won't do at all," said Edna. Albert thought she was going to pull the dog back but instead she took the can of soup out of his hand. "Look, Harvey. He was going to eat canned soup."

Harvey looked at the can. "I've got a pot of chili on now," he said. "Should be almost done. Why don't you join us for dinner?"

The couple didn't give Albert a chance to reply – Harvey grabbed his arm and led him over to their campsite.

He sat Albert at a wooden picnic table next to their camper. It was covered in a red and white checkered tablecloth anchored at each corner by an aluminum clip. In the center was a bright orange candle giving off a strange sweet smell. It made Albert's nose wrinkle.

"Keeps the bugs away," explained Edna. Albert looked around at the campsite. The table was positioned under an awning attached to the side of the camper. The area under the awning was covered with a rug made of fake plastic grass. Lights shaped like little lanterns were strung along the side of the camper and the awning.

"Homey, ain't it?" asked Edna. One of the light strings went off just as she said this.

"Darn it all," said Edna. "Must be a bulb. I'll take care of this. Albert, can you go into the camper and get the plastic forks? They're in a blue bin on the counter."

Albert opened his mouth to object but Edna had already shuffled off to repair the lights. Reluctantly he went into Harvey and Edna's camper to look for the forks.

He was searching for the container when he heard a voice behind him. "Excuse me sir?" it said.

"Yes," another similar voice interjected, "please help us."

Albert turned around to face the refrigerator. The voices were coming from a pair of pig-shaped refrigerator magnets. One of the pigs was clean and tidy, while the other was messy and dirty.

"It seems I'm on the refrigerator, but my job is to let you know when the dishes are clean," explained the tidy pig. "I should be on the dishwasher."

"You're always doing the talking," protested the other pig. "I say when the dishes are dirty. But I agree we can't do our job from here. Can you move us please?"

"I'm looking for the plastic forks," replied Albert. He was already nervous about wandering around in Harvey and Edna's camper without them.

"I don't even know the location of the dishwasher," said Albert. It wasn't just an excuse. He couldn't see anything that remotely looked like it could be a dishwasher.

"Don't listen to them partner," said a magnet of a cactus wearing a cowboy hat. "There ain't a dishwasher anywhere near these parts – unless you count the lady of the ranch."

"A dishwasher magnet with no dishwasher," lamented a moose magnet in a sullen voice. "Why is it even here? Why are any of us here?"

"Don't start that again," said an ice cream cone magnet holding a sign that read *We all scream for me!* "We don't need another existential discussion about the meaning of life."

"The meaning of life," began a magnet shaped like a short, overweight monk, "the meaning of life is to hang here and deliver our messages."

"Here we go," said the ice cream cone.

"God bless," continued the monk magnet, "I say... God bless...God bless this mess."

The moose magnet let out a large sigh. "Everything is a mess," he said.

"My mess...your mess...his mess...her mess," continued the monk. "As we hang here today, we must all testify to our mess. It is that mess...our personal mess...that defines us."

"He's on a roll now," said the ice cream cone with a sigh.

"It is a mess," proclaimed the monk, "but it is beautiful. And it is our mess. God bless...God bless this mess."

"Amen!" Shouted the cactus magnet.

"Hallelujah," said the pigs together.

"God bless this mess," repeated the monk.

"Amen," replied the moose in a resigned voice.

"God bless this mess," the monk said again.

Finally the ice cream cone agreed, "Amen. Plastic forks are in the blue container on the counter. Amen."

"Amen," said Albert as he quickly grabbed he blue container and headed back out of the camper.

Harvey set a large pot down on the table as Edna put out bowls and utensils. He ladled out a generous portion of chili for each of them.

"Dig in while it's still hot," said Harvey. "It's a culinary delight of the Midwest."

Albert tried the chili. It was actually quite delicious, much better than the canned soup he had planned to eat for dinner. Harvey looked at him expectantly so he nodded to indicate his enjoyment.

"You ain't much for talking, are you?" asked Edna.

"Leave him be," said Harvey. "He talks when he has something worth saying." Harvey leaned over closer to Albert. "Some people talk just to hear themselves," he said.

Albert nodded again, this time more slightly. Harvey condoning his silence actually made him feel more obligated to say something.

"I saw a bear today," announced Albert.

"In the campground?" asked Edna.

"Out on the trail," said Albert before taking another bite of chili.

"Close?" asked Harvey.

Albert nodded. "It was a mother with two cubs."

"Nothing more dangerous than a mother bear with her cubs," said Harvey. "What did you do?"

"I stood very still and waited," explained Albert. "It was almost an hour before the bears left."

"I bet it felt like six hours," said Harvey.

"That's why I stay off the trails," said Edna. "A bear could eat one of our babies."

Harvey rolled his eyes. "That and those dogs won't walk more than about fifteen feet before wanting you to pick them up."

They continued to eat and talk. Harvey and Edna related some of their camping experiences and Albert mostly talked about his walks. Eventually they came around to work and Albert explained the reason behind his travels.

"That must be so interesting to try out different things," said Edna.

Albert nodded. He told them about some of the other manuals he'd written over the past several years. He never thought anyone would be so interested in his work or that he'd enjoy talking about it so much.

13

Albert was enjoying the last of his morning coffee when there was a knock at the door. It was Harvey.

"Good morning Albert," he said. "I'll get right to the point. Have you ever played horseshoes?"

Albert admitted that he had not. "How about Bocce?" asked Harvey. Albert shook his head.

"Well you can learn as you go," replied Harvey. Before Albert could protest Harvey grabbed his arm and led him out of the motor coach and over to a grass lawn near their campsites.

"They have tournaments every weekend," explained Harvey. "Edna doesn't like to play…or leave the dogs. I was supposed to play with a fellow I met on the CB radio last week but he's got a busted fuel pump. I told him to get it looked at but he wouldn't listen. Now he's parked outside a supermarket waiting for a part."

As he spoke, Harvey continued to pull Albert along until they had reached a horseshoe pit. "I was about five minutes away from losing my spot when I said to myself: 'Self, you march right over and grab that nice fella Albert.' And then you know what?"

"You marched over and grabbed me?" said Albert.

"That's right," confirmed Harvey. "You stay here, I'll throw from the far side. We throw first." Harvey left Albert standing next to one of their opponents and walked to the other pit to join the second one.

"Just watch us," Harvey called out. "You'll pick it up in no time." Harvey and the other man began throwing the horseshoes. Harvey turned out to be a relatively skilled player, scoring a ringer and a leaner.

Albert picked up his horseshoes. "Howdy," said the first shoe. "Hey there," said the second. Albert remembered he had played a few times as a child, so he tried to recall the mechanics of the game.

His opponent gestured to him impatiently. Albert held the first horseshoe up. His hand was a bit shaky. "Settle down there son," said the horseshoe in his hand. "You're shaking more than a dog dunked in the rain trough."

Albert tried to relax his hand. "That's better," said the horseshoe. "Now square up with the stake." Albert did so. "Easier than shooting tin cans off the fence," said the horseshoe.

"Keep it nice and smooth," said the other horseshoe. "Like water off a duck's behind."

Albert swung his arm backward and then brought it forward, releasing the horseshoe just past his waist. It let out a "wahoo" as it flew through the air, followed by an "umph" as hit the ground. It landed a bit short, thudding into the sand a few inches in front of the stake.

"Nice throw," said his opponent.

"You're takin' to this like a horse to oats," encouraged Albert's other horseshoe.

Albert's opponent took his shot, which clanged off Albert's shoe and landed up against the stake. "That smarts," complained Albert's first horseshoe.

It was Albert's turn once again. He lined up with his second horseshoe. Albert eyed his target and threw harder this time. His strategy backfired and the horseshoe flew by the other horseshoes and the stake. It hit the grass behind the pit and went rolling.

"Whoa there hoss," called out the horseshoe. Albert blushed and shifted sheepishly to one side of the pit as the other pair retrieved the horseshoes.

"Shake it off, Albert," said Harvey. "That was a good throw, just not so hard next time." Harvey and his opponent took their turns. This time Harvey was unable to score any points so he and Albert fell further behind.

On the next round, Albert took his time and threw more carefully, winning the points. "Now you've got your scent on the trail," declared the first horseshoe. "Keep following the tracks," said the other.

Albert and Harvey managed to hold their own but the other players were clearly better. They lost the match fourteen points to twenty-one and were eliminated in the first around.

"Never fret much about losing a game," said one of the horseshoes. "Worry about losing the lesson."

"I'm sorry partner," said Harvey. "I thought we'd at least make it a couple of rounds. I let you down."

"Not at all," said Albert. "I enjoyed it." As he said the words, Albert realized he meant it.

"I'll make it up to you with some bocce," said Harvey and he led Albert over to the court.

A few moments later, Albert found himself throwing a large red ball at a smaller white one. Along the way it smacked into a green one. "Hey, I'm rollin' here!" it called out.

14

"Glad I could be of service for a change," said the clock radio as Albert pressed the off button for the alarm.

Albert went through his usual morning routine and ate a quick breakfast before starting to prepare the motor coach for travel.

"You're leaving?" asked the cell phone. "You were just starting to make friends."

"He's covered all the trails here," said the car keys. "It's time to move on to the next stop."

"Waterfalls next," said Albert.

"What about Harvey and Edna?" asked the cell phone. "They're organizing that pot luck for tomorrow night."

"I'm sure the dogs can keep them company," said the car keys. "It's time for Albert to get back on the road."

"Albert wants to visit the park with the waterfalls," added the reading glasses.

Albert finished the preparations for travel and said his goodbyes to Harvey and Edna. They were sorry to see him go but understood his desire to get back on the road. Harvey gave him his CB radio handle, adding the advice that Albert should really think about getting a CB radio. Edna gave him some food for the trip.

Albert was back on the road by mid-morning. The weather was clear and he was making fairly good time. Because he had studied the route the night before, he didn't use the navigation system on this leg of the trip. This allowed him to keep the display on the radio. Albert had recently written about that function so he now knew all of the stations available.

He was listening to a station that featured songs for the road when the display was suddenly interrupted by an incoming phone call. Albert had also discovered the steps to link his cell phone with the display. His brother's name and number were flashing on the screen. He tapped the answer button.

"Hello," said Albert.

"Albert?" called out his brother on the phone.

"Yes," said Albert.

"Albert, where are you?" asked his brother. "I went by your house the other day. Your car was there but no one answered."

"I'm on a trip," Albert replied. "In the motor coach, like I told you the last time we had lunch."

"You're actually doing that?" asked his brother. "You are driving a motor coach?"

"Yes," said Albert. "And I played bocce the other day."

"What?" asked his brother. "Never mind. When are you coming home, Albert?"

"I'm not sure," said Albert. "I'm on my way to a park with waterfalls."

"Waterfalls," said his brother. "What are you doing for money?"

"They're paying me," said Albert.

"Who's paying you?" asked his brother.

"The manufacturer of the motor coach," said Albert. "I'm writing a manual about it."

"Couldn't you just write about another toaster, Albert?" asked his brother. "I've been worried sick about you."

"Don't be worried," said Albert. "I'm learning all about it. I can back into a campsite, fill and empty all the tanks…"

"Are you at least using a navigation system?" asked his brother.

"Yes," said Albert. "I mean no…not this leg of the route. I studied the maps instead."

"That seems like a bad idea, Albert," said his brother. "You'll get lost and I'll have to come find you."

"I'm not going to get lost," said Albert. "I have maps and guides for the whole trip."

"I don't know about this," said his brother.

"Let's put him in the closet with the wallet," said the car keys.

"You should start screening your calls," said the cell phone.

"He is your brother," urged the reading glasses.

The call was beginning to make Albert nervous. All his doubts came flooding back. "I'll call you when I get to the next park," said Albert. "Goodbye."

Albert reached over and tapped the End Call button on the screen. The radio came back on and Albert began to sing along nervously.

15

A gleam on the horizon caught Albert's attention. A moment later, he was able to see it was some type of metal sculpture. Albert leaned forward to discover it was a vast group of sculptures someone had created from old scraps of metal. Albert decided he had to pull over and take a look. He parked the motor coach and walked to the front gate.

"Can I help you?" asked a voice inside. An elderly man stepped out from behind a chunk of metal.

"I saw your sculpture from the road and was wondering if I could take a look," replied Albert.

"Ain't nothin' here for sale," quipped the man.

"I was just going to look," said Albert.

"No charge for looking," said the man. "Come on in."

Albert went inside and found himself surrounded by all manner of objects and creatures constructed from various bits of discarded metal parts.

"I was a steering column from a sedan built in nineteen eighty three," said a long tube. "Now I'm part of a dragon."

"We're washing machine parts that have become part of a rocket," explained another group.

"I was a computer monitor," said a square box across the way. "Now I'm the body of a mouse."

"This was a good stop," said the reading glasses.

Albert nodded in agreement. "I don't think I'll ever look at an old appliance the same way."

"It's interesting," said the car keys, "but you should probably get back on the road if you want to make the next campsite before dark."

"You should talk to the owner more before you leave," suggested the cell phone. "I bet he has lots of stories to tell."

Albert took the old watch out of his pocket and stared at it. "The time is five thirty-six," it said. He was still looking at it when he heard a voice behind him.

"That's a nice piece," said the voice.

Albert turned around to find a short stocky woman wearing faded jeans and what looked to be a service station jacket from the nineteen fifties.

"My name is Ann," she continued. She handed Albert a piece of paper with a list on it. "I buy all sorts of things."

"My name is Albert," he replied and shook hands with the woman.

"How long have you had the watch?" asked Ann.

"Not long," said Albert. "I found it in the woods a few weeks ago."

"Would you consider selling it?" asked Ann.

Albert thought about this for a moment. "I'd like to learn more about," he said eventually.

"May I?" asked Ann. Albert handed her the watch. Ann gave it a long look. "I've seen this model around this area before. I try to buy them when I see them."

"So it's from this area?" asked Albert.

"Not exactly," replied Ann. "But a number of these made their way out here. They usually have an inscription. This one is unique though."

"Do you know who it might have belonged to?" asked Albert.

"I can't say," said Ann. "Any interest in selling it?"

Albert thought about this again. "I guess I was thinking I would like to get it back to the owner.

"I can respect that," said Ann. "Story of my day. This guy doesn't want to sell anything either," she said gesturing towards the owner of the sculpture garden. "I've been working on him all day. Won't even sell his extra parts."

"Sorry," said Albert.

"That's okay," said Ann. "Sometimes it's just about meeting people. "My name and number is on the paper there in case you change your mind."

Albert nodded and watched the woman walk away. She picked up a hood ornament from a pile nearby. "You have three of these," she started to say to the owner of the sculpture garden.'

"Not for sale," came the quick reply. Ann looked back at Albert and shrugged her shoulders. She gave him a final wave and headed toward the entrance of the garden.

Albert decided it was time he got back on the road as well. He still wanted to stop and withdraw some money before he arrived at the next campground. Albert thanked the sculptor at the gate on the way out and returned to the motor coach.

16

Albert pulled into the parking lot of the bank and maneuvered the motor coach into two back to back parking spaces. He got out and walked over to the entrance. Albert pulled on the door but it was locked.

"You have to put your debit card into the slot to unlock the door," explained the reading glasses.

Albert put his card into the slot and heard a click. He opened the door and went into the vestibule of the bank. The ATM machine was at the far end. Albert walked over to it and inserted his card.

"Good evening," said the ATM. "Please choose a language."

"English," said Albert tapping the corresponding button.

"Would you like to set this language as your default setting?" Asked the ATM.

"Yes," said Albert and he tapped the button.

"Would you like to open a CD today?" asked the ATM.

"No," said Albert.

"What would you like to do next?" Asked the ATM. "View your balance? Make a withdrawal? Make a deposit? Other?"

Albert was somewhat curious about the "other" category but was in too much of a hurry to try it. He clicked the button to view his balance.

"Loading," the ATM responded. "While I'm retrieving you information, would you like to hear more about our vehicle loans?"

"No," Albert said flatly. "I would like to know my balance."

A moment later the ATM displayed his balance on the screen. "Would you like a printed copy of your balance?" asked the ATM.

"No," said Albert.

"What would you like to do next?" asked the ATM.

Albert tapped the button to make a withdrawal.

"I can help you with that today," said the ATM. "How much would you like to take out?"

Albert inputted a number and a moment later some bills slid out of the machine.

"Please take your cash," said the ATM machine. "Do you want to conduct another transaction?"

"No," said Albert. He pressed the exit button and put the cash and debit card inside his pocket. He turned and started to leave the vestibule.

"Would you like to hear about our CDs?" the ATM asked from behind him. Albert turned back toward the ATM.

"Did you know that we also offer several investment options?" continued the ATM. "Schedule an appointment today to learn more."

"No thank you," said Albert. He started to walk away.

"Student loans," said the ATM. "I can help you consolidate your student loans."

"I paid those off already," said Albert. He turned around to leave again.

"Home mortgage? Additional insurance? Christmas Club?" The ATM shouted out.

"No thank you," said Albert. He walked quickly to the door and the vestibule. A moment later he was back on the road.

Albert was surprised at how quickly the light faded once he began driving again. He'd made himself a sandwich to eliminate the need to make a dinner stop but that only helped a little. His visit to the sculpture garden had put him well behind schedule.

"You may want to go a little faster," suggested the car keys. "You don't want to get there too late."

"This is a good safe speed," said the reading glasses. "No need to drive unsafe."

"And he could always find a spotter when he gets there," added the cell phone.

Albert saw a sign for gas off the next exit. He looked down at the gauge. There was enough fuel to make it to his next campsite, so he decided to keep going rather than lose more time.

"That is a good decision," said the car keys. "You don't want to lose any more time."

Albert watched the last bit of daylight fade away. Time on the road passed more slowly in the dark. There was nothing to see except for the lines and reflectors lit by the headlights. Albert was glad he'd gotten a good night's sleep. Otherwise he thought he might have nodded off.

"You could always stay at a hotel and continue in the morning," suggested the reading glasses. "There's one at the next exit."

"There's one at every exit," said the car keys. "It's still early. He has time to get to the campground."

The hotel was a reasonable idea but he couldn't shake the nagging feeling it would be like giving up or taking a step backward. He had parked the motor coach in the dark before. Tonight would be later but certainly not any darker.

Albert thought about the recent conversation with his brother. "Imagine if he knew how far I've driven," said Albert. "And the things I've done."

"That's right Albert," said the car keys. "Don't prove him right. Keep going. It's still early."

"You could call someone," suggested the cell phone. "That would pass the time."

Albert liked the idea but was unsure who he could call from the motor coach. He certainly didn't want to talk to his brother again and Harvey had only given him his CB handle. He thought about calling the woman he'd met earlier in the day. Albert decided that would be odd since he didn't really know her.

Staring at the two beams in front of him, he started thinking about the lights on the motor coach. "The Venture features a full range of navigational and functional lighting," said Albert. "In addition to its powerful headlights, it includes fog lights, marker lights and running lights." Albert felt a little better. He sat back in his seat and forged ahead.

PART 4

1

Albert squinted his eyes to get a better look at the approaching overhead signs. The highway was splitting ahead and he needed to make the correct choice. He believed he needed to bear to the left of the split but he wanted to make sure before hitting that point.

"What about the navigation?" asked the cell phone.

"It's too dangerous to punch in the information now," said the reading glasses. It would be distracted driving."

Albert couldn't argue with that. He made his way into the left lane and stayed to the left during the split. Almost immediately the road appeared to split again. Albert didn't recall seeing that on the map but continued to bear left.

A sharp curve in the road gave Albert a sinking feeling in the pit of his stomach. He may have made a wrong turn or he might just be second guessing himself. It seemed like he was still going in the right direction. He knew he had to make right turn at an upcoming intersection. He remembered seeing railroad tracks on the map.

A moment later he did indeed go over railroad tracks. Confidence restored, he went right at the following light. After the turn there should have been a river to his left and a small town. Instead he passed briefly through an industrial area followed only by an area of dense trees. The sinking feeling returned.

At this point Albert was almost sure he'd made a wrong turn somewhere. He wanted to pull over and start the navigation system, but there was no shoulder on either side of the road.

Albert looked at the compass on the dashboard. It was flipping between north and northeast depending on the current curvature of the road. He knew he should be going due east, so he reasoned his direction wasn't entirely off. Albert reasoned he should cross one of the major highways sooner or later.

He went back to reciting the information about the motor coach's lighting features to distract him from his building anxiety. "The Venture features a full range of navigational and functional lighting," said Albert. "In addition to its powerful headlights, it includes fog lights, marker lights and running lights."

A short time later Albert passed a small sign mentioning the park that was his destination. He followed the sign and turned down a smaller road. "This is probably a smaller entrance on the other side," he said out loud.

"The gas gauge is getting lower," warned the reading glasses. Albert looked down and was surprised to see how quickly the needle had dropped. It seemed like the gauge hadn't moved in miles. Now all of a sudden it was down below the quarter tank marker.

"You can't continue much further, Albert," said the reading glasses.

"It might be good to stop for the night somewhere," conceded the car keys.

"There's almost no signal," said the cell phone. Albert gave the screen a quick glance. There was only one bar on the display.

The road he was on eventually gave way to an even smaller one. Albert eased the motor coach onto it and knew for sure something was very wrong. This road was extremely bumpy. It even rocked the Venture's "advanced suspension system designed to provide a car-like ride on any road conditions."

"This is as dirt road," said the reading glasses. "That's why the motor coach is bouncing around so much."

The entire right front side of the vehicle lurched downward and then bounced back up again, followed by the right rear. Albert held his breath, worried he had blown a tire.

"Professional grade tires that are reinforced with run flat technology that will keep you going in even the harshest conditions," Albert murmured. He trained the corner of his eye on the dashboard waiting for the low tire warning to appear.

When the warning did not appear after several minutes, Albert led out a sigh of relief. He leaned forward and looked through the large windows at the road ahead. Everything was pitch black except for the headlight beams. They revealed nothing but gravel and pine branches. He saw no signs of civilization on the horizon or above the tops of the trees.

"You have to stop somewhere," said the reading glasses.

"I don't know where to stop," said Albert.

"Turn around," suggested the car keys.

"There isn't enough room," Albert replied. The road had narrowed so much that the motor coach itself barely fit between the sides of it.

Not long after, the engine of the motor coach began to stutter and lose power. Albert looked at the gas gauge and saw the needle had now fallen below the empty line. It didn't take long for the vehicle's large engine to sip out the remaining drops of fuel.

"The Venture's eight cylinder engine provides enough power to move you and all your provisions to the next destination," said Albert.

"As long as you have fuel," added the car keys.

2

Albert sat at the table of the motor coach and stared at the darkness surrounding him. He had most of the lights turned off. The Venture had auxiliary batteries but he was worried about draining them too quickly. Albert turned away from the window and put his head in his hands. He was completely lost.

He imagined his brother's reaction. "I knew this would happen. You're lost in the woods somewhere. Now I'll need to lead a search party to find you."

"Don't worry about his reaction," said the cell phone. "You can't call him anyway. No service at all now." Albert looked down at the phone. There were no bars.

"I am all alone out here," said Albert. Then another thought occurred to him. "What if I'm not all alone?"

He leapt up from the table and went around locking all the doors and windows in the motor coach.

"You should eat something," said the reading glasses. "Drink some water. You'll feel better."

Albert wasn't feeling hungry or thirsty but got up and retrieved a bottle of water from the refrigerator. The refrigerator worked on propane so the water was still cold. He found the water helped a bit so he decided to make himself a peanut butter sandwich. At the very least, eating served as a momentary distraction.

After his meal, Albert started pacing the length of the motor coach. His brother's reaction was the least of his problems. He had no idea of his location. He was out of gas. He had limited food. He didn't even own the motor coach.

"Walking back and forth isn't helping," said the car keys. "You need to figure out what to do next."

"I have to agree," said the reading glasses. "You're only getting yourself more worked up."

Albert flopped into a chair. He was completely exhausted. "Maybe I just need to get some sleep," he said.

"Good idea," agreed the reading glasses. "Everything will look better after a good night's sleep."

Albert skipped his usual nighttime routine and didn't even bother to change clothes. He simply walked to the bedroom and dropped onto the bed. Albert slept on top of the sheets. He fell asleep quickly but he did not sleep well.

In his dreams he was driving the motor coach. Even though he took all the right turns he would still get lost. Or he would see the light of a town on the horizon but never reach it. In another variation Albert found himself at a gas station but no fuel would come out of the pump.

Other times he would dream that he was back in the campgrounds or hiking along the trails, only to wake up still lost in the woods. For Albert, the only thing worse than the dreams was thinking about his current situation. For that reason, each time he woke up he would roll back over and go back to sleep – no matter how disturbing or disappointing the previous dream.

In the early hours of the morning his exhaustion took over and Albert finally fell into a deep enough sleep that he no longer dreamed.

3

It was extremely bright when Albert woke up the next morning. He hadn't closed the bedroom curtains so light was streaming into the motor coach. For a brief moment he completely forgot about the events of the previous evening, clinging to the idea he'd never left the previous campground. Then it all came rushing back to him – the wrong turns, getting lost, running out of gas.

Albert went into the bathroom and splashed some water on his face. He went through an abridged version of his morning routine before taking a look outside. Albert hoped he could get his bearings once he saw his current surroundings. He unlocked the side door of the motor coach and stepped out.

He immediately fell to the ground in a heap. Disoriented, Albert picked himself up off the ground and looked back. The step under the door was a mangled wreck. Albert remembered the motor coach lurching violently to the right the night before. He hadn't blown a tire but he had destroyed the step.

Albert tried to pull the step back into shape but it wouldn't budge. He sighed and decided he should check over the rest of the Venture to see if there was any other damage. He made a slow pass along each side of the vehicle, paying special attention to the wheels and bumpers. Everything looked okay except for the step. This gave him at least a small degree of comfort.

After giving the motor coach a once over, Albert took a closer look at his surroundings. The road appeared to be well maintained but relatively untraveled.

The edges had been recently trimmed. However, there were no tire tracks and the ruts were not deep. Thick forest surrounded the road on either side. There were no powerlines or any other signs of infrastructure.

Albert made his way back to the front of the motor coach and walked a short way down the road to see if he could spot anything. He found only more road and trees. It reminded him of the Sunday morning cartoons he'd watched as a kid where the characters would keep passing the same rock or tree over and over again.

He walked to the rear of the motor coach and checked the road in that direction. It was the same result – nothing but the gravel of the road and trees on either side. At this point, Albert was extremely thirsty so he went back inside the Venture to get a drink.

He retrieved a bottle of water from the refrigerator and sat down at the kitchen table. After several long gulps he decided to check the maps. Albert reasoned that if he could figure out his wrong turns he could make out his current position.

Albert took out the maps and laid them on the table. He traced the highlighted route with his finger until he reached the point where the main highway split. He knew he'd initially gone to the left. That road should have taken him almost directly to the campground. It had several natural curves to the left. It also had several smaller roads that split off to the left.

Albert realized he must have taken one of those smaller roads, rather than simply following the natural curve of the main road. There were only two possible turns he could have taken but he also made several other turns after his initial mistake. Albert took a pencil and drew a circle on the map. The circle was relatively large and most of it was forest.

He stared at that circle for a long time, trying to recall his exact sequence of turns. Nothing seemed to match up exactly. Sooner or later he'd end up in the middle of the woods. Albert knew he was probably misjudging the time between turns.

"Or worse," he said out loud, "this road isn't on any of the maps."

4

"You have to come up with a plan, Albert," said the car keys.

"He knows that," said the reading glasses. "He's just taking his time."

"If he keeps taking his time," replied the car keys, "he'll eventually run out of food or water."

"He has two cases of bottled water," said the cell phone, "plus the water in the holding tank."

"He'd be out of this mess by now if you were any help," accused the car keys.

"It's not my fault I have no signal," lamented the cell phone. "He should have stayed in better contact with people."

"I should have done that," agreed Albert.

"There's also plenty of peanut butter and jelly and oriental noodles," said the reading glasses.

"The generator runs on gasoline," said the car keys. "What if you siphoned gas out of that tank and put it into the regular fuel tank?"

"Then I could get the motor coach moving again," said Albert. "I might be able to drive out of this."

"The generator has a small tank," said the reading glasses. "And you don't know how far you'd have to go to get out. Then we'd be stuck with only the batteries and propane."

Albert had to agree with this assessment. A couple of gallons of gas might only get him twenty or so miles. That might not be enough to get out.

"How far did you come on this road?" asked the cell phone.

Albert wasn't sure. Even if he could get the motor coach turned around, he might not have enough gas to get back to the previous road.

"And you don't know what may or may not be on that previous road," said the reading glasses.

"Do you even know how to siphon gas?" asked the cell phone.

Albert shook his head. That seemed to put an end to the discussion about moving fuel. He wasn't sure if he had the right equipment to do it, if he could figure out how to do it, or if it would even work.

"Too bad," said the cell phone. "Would have made an interesting chapter in the manual."

"That's not really helpful," said the reading glasses.

"I'm using humor to diffuse a tense situation," replied the cell phone.

Albert took the old watch out of his pocket and looked at it. "The time is two thirty-six," it said.

Albert threw it across the motor coach. It made a loud bang as it hit the front window of the vehicle. He immediately regretted throwing the watch and got up to retrieve it. Albert had to search around to find it. Eventually he located it under the passenger seat. There was a large crack across the face.

"The time is two thirty-seven," it said.

Albert was more disappointed with himself than he'd ever been in his life, including that day at the beach with his brother. He ran his fingers over the face of the watch as tears rolled down his cheeks.

"You can get it fixed," suggested the reading glasses.

"Anything can be fixed," said the deep voice.

Albert looked up. "What?" he asked.

"Anything can be fixed," the voice said again.

"How?" asked Albert.

"You have to answer that for yourself," replied the deep voice.

Albert slumped down in the passenger seat of the motor coach. He wiped the tears from his face and looked at the watch again.

"The time is two forty-one," it said.

Albert walked back to the table and looked at the maps. "I'm going to have to walk out," he said. "There's no other way. I have to walk out and get fuel and help."

"Someone will probably have to drive you back to the motor coach," said the cell phone.

"I might also get to a place with cell phone reception," said Albert.

"Right," agreed the cell phone. "And then you could call someone."

"I can call someone for help," said Albert. He looked at the watch again.

"The time is two forty-six," it said.

"Still five hours of day light left," said the car keys.

"I'll go tomorrow," said Albert." "That would be the safer choice.

"For what it's worth, I agree," came a muffled voice from the closet. It was the wallet.

5

The next morning Albert had a light breakfast before starting out. He'd prepared a backpack with several bottles of water and some sandwiches. He opened the door to the motor coach and stepped out onto a crate he'd placed there to take the place of the broken step.

Albert looked to right and then to the left. He had to decide which way to go – back towards the previous road or forward toward wherever this road might lead.

"You should go forward, Albert," declared the car keys.

"It might be better to retrace your route back to the previous road," said the reading glasses.

"I recommend you take another look at the maps," said the wallet. Albert had taken it out of the closet and was carrying it again.

"Remember the compass, Albert?" said the car keys. "It was pointing the correct general direction when you were driving. Going back would be the wrong direction."

"And if anyone would know about wrong directions…" said the wallet.

"And there it is," said the car keys.

"What?" asked the wallet.

"The I told you so," said the car keys. "I knew you couldn't resist."

"This isn't helping," said the reading glasses.

Albert put his hand up against his forehead to shield against the sun. He stared at the road ahead of the motor coach. Then he turned backward and looked at the road behind him. Both views seemed almost exactly the same.

"It might not matter," said the cell phone. "There may be service in either direction."

"You studied the maps, Albert," said the wallet. "If you're not going to take the time to look at them again, at least think about what you observed on them."

"How is that going to help?" asked the car keys. "There are only two directions. Unless he goes through the woods."

"Based on the maps," explained the wallet, "are you most likely closer to another road or town ahead of you or behind you?"

Albert thought about this. "I have a better chance if I walk forward," he decided. "I didn't see much along the road the last hour I was driving."

Resigned to this decision, Albert started walking down the road ahead of the motor coach. Two hours later he stopped to rest. He sat down on a fallen log by the side of the road. After taking a drink he looked at the way ahead and the way behind. There was still almost no difference between the two.

"Maybe this was the wrong direction," said the reading glasses.

"It's only been a couple of hours," said the car keys. "He probably hasn't gone that far yet."

"The average person walks between two and three miles per hour," said the wallet. "Albert's kept up a pretty good pace so it's probably been around five miles."

"How do you know that?" asked the cell phone.

"Albert worked on that manual for the pedometer last year," said the wallet.

"That's right," said the reading glasses. "I wish he had that pedometer now."

"Press on, Albert," recommended the car keys. "You have to be close. How far could this road go?"

"That's the problem," said the wallet. "He doesn't know how far this road goes. It could be miles and miles."

"Based on the maps I should cross another road at some point," said Albert. "All the roads on the map intersected other roads at some point."

"At what point?" asked the wallet. "Ten miles…fifteen miles…twenty miles?"

"I don't know how far it might be," said Albert.

"Do you remember the scale of the maps?" asked the wallet. Albert could not recall the scale of the maps.

"Maybe you should have gone the other way," said the reading glasses.

"Well he's going this way now," snapped the car keys. "It would be counter-productive to turn back and go the other way now."

Albert sighed and continued down the road. An hour later he stopped again to eat a sandwich. He wasn't very hungry but knew he should eat something. Collapsing out here away from the motor coach would make the situation a hundred times worse. He surveyed the road around him while he ate.

"It's still the same," said the wallet. "You don't seem any closer to anything."

"This is bad," Albert concluded. "What if I can't walk out of this?"

"You just have to keep going," encouraged the cell phone. "You'll find someone."

"This isn't working," said the wallet. "You should go back and re-examine your options."

"No," protested the car keys. "There could be something or someone right around the next bend. The only thing behind you is a motor coach that's out of gas."

"If I turn back now," said Albert. "It would be a waste of the whole day."

"You can only go on for so long," said the reading glasses. "Otherwise you'll be too tired to walk all the way back."

Albert had to admit this was true. He had walked three hours almost non-stop. If he did not reach something soon, he'd have to return to the motor coach. Otherwise he might end up spending the night out here.

"It may be more than one day's walk to get out of here," said the wallet.

The idea it might take more than a day to walk out had never occurred to Albert.

"I have no idea what might be out there," he said waving his hand at the woods. He thought about the bear and her cubs. Albert heard the cracking of a branch behind him.

He jumped up from his resting place and began to walk again. "I'll go for another hour or so," he said. "If I haven't found anything I'll turn back."

Albert took another drink of water and continued to walk. An hour and a half later he stopped, flopping down on the gravel along the side of the road. He lay down on his back and stared up at the clouds. One of them reminded him of a horseshoe and that got him thinking about playing horseshoes and bocce with Harvey.

"You should have just stayed there," said the wallet. "It was safe."

"And you were making friends," sighed the cell phone.

"Give it another half hour," suggested the car keys.

"That's not a good idea," said the reading glasses. "You're not prepared to spend the night out here."

"True," Albert agreed.

"You don't have enough food or water to spend the night," said the reading glasses. "Or even a blanket."

"The temperature will most likely drop out here at night," added the wallet.

Albert got up off the ground. He took a last look at the road ahead of him before turning around and starting the long walk back to the motor coach.

6

After having another peanut butter and jelly sandwich for dinner, Albert spent an hour studying the maps. He retraced all the routes again, trying to pinpoint his location.

"It doesn't make sense," said Albert. "It's as if this road doesn't even exist."

"Maybe this road isn't on the map," suggested the reading glasses.

"That's unlikely," said the wallet. "You should get a good night's sleep and spend tomorrow studying the maps again."

"Enough with the maps," said the car keys. "Maybe you should revisit the plan to siphon the gasoline."

"Not that half-baked plan again," said the wallet.

"Or maybe you should build a fire," said the cell phone. "That might attract someone's attention."

"Starting a fire might not be a bad idea," said Albert.

"With lots of smoke," suggested the cell phone.

"A fire out here would be very dangerous," said the wallet. "Don't forget about the root fire."

"There are no roots in the road," said the car keys.

"You can't be sure of that, Albert," said the wallet. "You're surrounded by trees and bushes. It wouldn't be hard for a spark to start a forest fire."

"It might be worth the risk," said the cell phone. "You need help, Albert."

Albert thought about this. A fire might bring help right away, but it could also cause bigger problems. He might even get in trouble for starting the fire. He didn't want to make things any worse.

"Starting a fire is always an option," said the reading glasses. "But it's only one option."

"Exactly," said the car keys. "You should try to walk out again, Albert."

"Where are you going to go?" asked the wallet. "Which direction?"

"It's obvious," said the car keys. "Tomorrow you should try to walk back the way you came."

"This morning you told him to go forward," said the wallet. "Don't go backward," the wallet mocked in its best imitation the car keys.

"Let's study the maps for another eight hours," answered the car keys in its best imitation of the wallet.

"Please stop fighting," requested the reading glasses.

"Yes," added the cell phone. "And neither of you does a good impression."

Albert looked down at the maps and decided there was nothing more that he could learn from them. One by one he folded them up and placed them back in the drawer, except for a map of his immediate area. He placed that map in his backpack.

"Tomorrow I'll try going the other direction," said Albert.

"And go as far as it takes," suggested the car keys.

"I'll walk for up to four hours," corrected Albert. "If I don't find anything in that direction I'll turn back and spend the night in the motor coach.

"And what then, Albert?" asked the wallet.

Albert did not reply. He just stood and stared at the woods through the kitchen window in silence.

7

Perhaps from the sheer exhaustion of a long day's walk, Albert slept deeply and woke up extremely refreshed. He packed his bag again with sandwiches, water and some extra clothes just in case. He stepped outside and without any debate this time, began to walk down the road behind the motor coach.

"Everything looks the same this direction too," observed the reading glasses.

"Still no service," added the cell phone.

"It hasn't been that long," said the car keys. "Just keep moving forward, Albert."

"I thought we were going backward today," said the wallet.

"Don't get technical," replied the car keys.

"Getting technical is my job," said the wallet. "What happens if you don't find anything today, Albert?"

"I'm not sure what I'll do if I don't come across anything this time," said Albert. "I suppose I either need to start a fire or pack more and keep walking until I find something."

"Are you prepared for any of those things?" asked the wallet.

"You can cross that bridge when you come to it Albert," suggested the car keys. "No sense worrying about it now."

"Fine," said the wallet. "What happens if you find a way out today, Albert? What then?"

"Then he's out of the woods," said the cell phone. "Literally."

"Exactly," agreed the car keys.

"You'll be safe again," added the reading glasses.

"What comes next?" pressed the wallet. "Will you go home after that?"

The question caught Albert off guard. The last couple days he'd thought only about getting the motor coach back to civilization. He hadn't even considered whether he would continue on from here or just return home.

"You have more than enough experience to finish the manual," said the wallet. "I think this has already been plenty of adventure. You even played bocce…not too well of course, but you did it."

"This is just a detour," said the car keys. "Albert will be back on track in no time."

"And meeting more people," added the cell phone.

"It might be nice to be home again," said the reading glasses. "You could take another trip some other time."

"Yes," said the wallet. "Find your way out of this Albert and then head home."

"Or he could put you back in the closet," said the car keys.

"And how did that work out last time?" asked the wallet.

Albert decided it was time for a break. He leaned against a tree and took out a bottle of water. He splashed some on his face and took a long drink. Albert looked at the old watch. He'd been walking for over an hour.

"Everything still looks the same," said the reading glasses.

"I know it all looks the same," said Albert. The scenery no longer reminded him of those old cartoons. It was like some B grade science fiction movie where the main character was trapped in some kind of void…or perhaps his own mind.

"Keep moving, Albert," said the car keys. "You only have so much time."

Albert started walking again. He kept his head down, barely looking from side to side anymore. The good memories of the trip seemed far away now. It was like he had always been in these woods, dealing with these problems.

"Does any of this look familiar Albert?" asked the reading glasses. "A curve in the road, maybe?"

"Or a rut on the road," said Albert. Looking down for the past mile or so made it easy for him to spot a large dent in the road. He walked up to it and knelt down at the edge.

"This is where I crushed the step," he said.

Albert wasn't able to determine anything about his position from the rut, but it still made him feel a bit better. It meant he wasn't in some void or dark part of his mind.

"Do you remember how long you hit the rut after turning off the main road?" asked the reading glasses.

"I don't remember," said Albert.

"This means you're making progress towards the previous road," said the car keys. "Move on before it gets too late."

"You can't be sure there was anything to find on the previous road either," said the wallet.

"There may be service," said the cell phone.

Albert continued down the road with renewed energy. He walked for another two hours.

"It's starting to get late," said the reading glasses.

"This could be my best chance," said Albert. He walked on for another hour. However, he did not reach the other road.

"The other road could still be miles ahead," said the wallet. "You drove in…you're walking now."

"You could also be really close," said the car keys.

"Albert, if you don't turn back now you won't get back to the motor coach before dark," said the wallet.

"And you may be too tired to make it back if you go any further," added the reading glasses.

Albert wanted to keep going, but he knew he wasn't ready to sleep in the woods. Disappointed, he turned around and headed back to the motor coach for a second time.

8

The next morning Albert packed even more into his backpack. He made sure he had enough to sustain an overnight stay in the woods. In addition to food and extra clothes, he packed a blanket, rain tarp and first aid kit. Albert hoped he wouldn't have to stay more than one night outside the motor coach.

"That pack is getting heavier," said the car keys. "Do you really need all that stuff?"

"Of course he does," interjected the wallet.

"It might weight you down," replied the car keys.

"He needs the essentials," said the reading glasses. "He's not camping out in the backyard."

Albert stepped outside of the motor coach and looked up and down the road. "You should go the same route as yesterday," said the wallet. "Remember the rut. You were at least on the right path to the previous road."

"You don't know how far past that rut you need to go," said the car keys. "I think you should go forward again."

"First you say to go forward," said the wallet. "Then you say to go back. Now it's forward again.

"I'm simply assessing the situation day by day," said the car keys.

"You should go backward, Albert," said the wallet.

"Head towards your destination," argued the car keys. "That's forward, not back."

"That destination doesn't matter," said the wallet. "He's going home after this."

"He never said he was going home after this," protested the car keys. "Did you, Albert?"

"It's the right decision," said the wallet.

"This is making a bad situation worse," said the reading glasses.

"Forward!" Shouted the car keys.

"Back!" The wallet yelled in return.

"Make a decision, Albert," urged the cell phone.

"I've made a decision," said Albert. He turned and went back into the motor coach. Once inside, he took the wallet out of his pocket and set it on the table. He removed his driver's license, some cash and a credit card. He placed these items back in his pocket.

"Excellent," said the car keys. "I knew you'd make the right decision, Albert."

Next Albert took the motor coach's door key off the ring with the car keys and put it in his other pocket. He hung the car keys on a hook in the kitchen. "Wait a second, Albert," said the keys. "Let's talk about this."

Albert checked the service on his cell phone. There were still no bars so he shut the cell phone off and placed it in his pack. He took his reading glasses from around his neck and placed them in their case. Albert put the case into the pocket with the map.

Lastly, he looked down at the old watch. "The time is eight twelve," it said. Albert put the watch back in his pocket. He swung the backpack over his shoulders and walked back out of the motor coach. He locked the door and at the road again.

Albert decided it probably didn't matter which way he went on the road. He also reasoned it probably wasn't worth spending more than one night away from the motor coach. If he couldn't reach anything in two days he should probably just light a fire, regardless of the risk.

"If I light a fire in the middle of the road and be extra careful, I should be able to contain it," Albert said to no one in particular.

He stood thinking about that for a moment. "The road should contain the fire," he repeated. The feeling that came over him next was a mixture of relief and disappointment at his own stupidity.

"This is a fire break." Albert practically yelled the words. "That's why it's not on the map. I turned onto a fire break by mistake."

Albert stood quietly for several moments. He heard the sounds of the forest for the first time, the same way he heard them on his nature walks. There were the calls of birds, chirping of insects and the wind rustling through the trees. Except the more he listened, the more Albert didn't think he was hearing the wind at all.

"That's water," he concluded. Albert set his backpack on the ground and took out the map. There were no fire breaks on it but there were several streams. Albert held onto the map and slid the pack onto his back.

He took a deep breath and walked right into the forest, heading in the direction of the sound of the water. Albert paused several feet in, realizing that he might need a way back to the motor coach. He started arranging sticks on the ground into arrows every so often.

Albert was surprised to learn just how far the sound of the water could carry through the woods. It took him almost an hour to reach the stream. He was so grateful he bent down and splashed the water on his face. Then he consulted the map. It was hard to match this stream exactly with one on the map. He did have a general idea of his potential position along each stream, though.

Albert could tell that if he made a left turn along almost any of the creeks, he'd eventually reach a road or some type of facility. He gathered some sticks into a very large arrow pointing back towards the motor coach. Then he turned left and started making his way along the water.

An hour and a half later Albert was sure the forest was beginning to thin out. More and more daylight was breaking through the tops of the pines. He paused briefly to take a drink of water and then pressed on along the creek. Not much later he heard another familiar sound.

Albert smiled widely. "That was the sound of a car," he announced. Then he heard the sound again...and again. He stumbled further up the creek and after a few minutes he could see the gleam of a culvert above the creek. Albert emerged along side a well travelled road.

He took off his pack and got out the cell phone. While it was powering up, Albert looked down the road and saw he was only about seventy feet away from a general store. Parked in front of it was a forest ranger's pickup truck.

9

Albert stumbled his way into the parking lot just as the park ranger was leaving the general store.

"You look like you could use some help," she said. The ranger held out her hand to Albert and he shook it. "I'm Ranger McCarin but most people around here just call me Ranger Sally or just plain old Sally."

Albert didn't think there was anything plain about her. "My name is Albert," he replied. "I got lost the other night."

"Let me guess," said Sally. "You're parked in that fire lane back there a ways."

Albert shook his said. "I'm so sorry to be a problem," he said.

"Don't worry a bit about it," replied Sally. "I've been on the state to mark those roads better. We get four or five campers lost on that lane every season."

"I tried to walk along the road for a couple of days," explained Albert. "Then I realized I was in the fire break. That's when I made for the creek."

"Well good for you," said Sally. "Most people just start a fire. We even had one fella' tried to burn his spare tire. He figured it would make more smoke."

"I figured a fire would be dangerous," said Albert.

"You got that right," said Sally. She led him into the general store. "Jack..." she called out. "This is Albert. He spent a few nights stuck out on that fire break. Get him a plate of your chicken and dumplings and a piece of whatever pie you've got today."

Jack, who Albert reasoned was the general store owner, set a out plate of food on a small counter with a three stools in front of it. "On the house," he said. "You start on that and I'll get you a cup of coffee."

"Go ahead and get some hot food into you," said Sally. "After you eat I'll drive you back to your vehicle. I assume you'll need some fuel. I always keep a can in the back of my truck."

Albert nodded again as he started eating the chicken and dumplings. It was the first hot food he'd eaten in almost three days. He finished quickly and then gulped down the coffee.

"How was it?" asked Jack.

"Very good," said Albert. "Thank you very much."

"You're welcome," said Jack. "I also keep the store pretty well stocked. Need anything besides gas?"

"I banged up my step," said Albert.

"I don't have steps," said Jack, "but I've got a good selection of tools. Take a look around before you head out."

Albert nodded and strolled around. He couldn't believe how good it felt just to be back in a store again.

He came across an aisle with a wide variety of toys. There were toys that could be played in the car, sand toys for use at the lake, and several other categories packed into a remarkably small space.

"You need a hug," said a stuffed bear.

"No thank you," replied Albert.

"A hug?" shouted a plastic toy soldier. "You need to toughen up son. Your momma isn't here to clean and dress you. Make yourself presentable for inspection."

Albert spotted a play make-up kit and used the mirror to look at his appearance. He was very disheveled from his hike along the creek. His shirt was untucked and there was dirt on his face. Albert glanced back at the female ranger talking to the store owner. He tucked in his shirt and used his sleeve to wipe the dirt off his face.

"That's better," said the toy soldier. "Now get yourself together."

"You still need a hug," said the bear.

"No thank you," said Albert. He wondered whether he should buy something for his nieces while he was here. Then he realized he wasn't sure of their ages.

"Everyone likes a doll," said a fashion doll on the lower shelf.

"Why not buy two," added a similar doll in a different outfit.

"Stop worrying about dolls and bears and get your head into the game son," shouted the toy soldier.

Albert nodded.

"Are you a bird dipping your head into the water for insects?" asked the toy soldier.

Albert shook his head.

"Then what do you have to say for yourself?" asked the toy solider.

Albert thought for a moment. "Sir, yes sir," he said.

"That's better solider," said the toy soldier. "Now stop fiddling around in this aisle and get back to the counter."

Albert heard a familiar voice call out his name. He looked around for the source. It wasn't Sally or Jack. They were talking to each other over by the counter.

"Albert it's me," said the voice. It was coming from the end of the aisle. Albert made his way towards the voice, only to find a postcard rack.

"It is you," said the voice. "Down here, Albert."

Albert looked down at the lowest level of the rack. There he found a postcard imprinted with The Scream. He picked it up off the rack.

"How are you, Albert?" asked the painting.

"Better now," Albert replied. "I was lost in the woods for awhile."

"But you're safe now?" asked the painting.

"Yes," said Albert.

"How has the trip been otherwise?" It asked.

Albert thought for a moment. "Good," he said. "It's been good."

"Are you glad you took the trip?" asked the painting.

"I am," said Albert.

"Ready to go?" asked Sally walking towards him. Albert nodded.

"You can keep that postcard if you want," said Jack. "It's been on that rack for years."

"Thank you," said Albert. He turned the postcard over. The words "WHAT DO YOU MEAN I HAVE TO TAKE A VACATION?" were printed on the back.

10

It was late in the afternoon by the time Albert pulled into the campground. The ranger had driven him back to his vehicle and then lead him out of the fire break to the nearest gas station. After Albert filled his tanks, he followed her to the campground. By that time Albert had calmed down enough to do a fairly good job backing in the motor coach.

"You look like you've been driving that rig for years," said Sally. "It looks new, though. How long have you had it?"

"Just a couple of weeks," explained Albert. "I'm writing the manual for the manufacturer."

"That must be interesting work," said Sally. "And fun, I imagine."

"Sometimes," said Albert.

"When you're not out of gas in a fire break," said Sally.

"Yes," said Albert. "Thank you again for helping me."

"You're welcome," said Sally. "That's my job. I've wanted to be a ranger ever since I was a little girl."

"I always wanted to be a writer," said Albert. "And I'm good with things."

"You must have a way," said Sally, "if you learned to handle this machine that fast. She is a beauty. Do you have to give it back?"

Albert hadn't thought about this. He was so caught up in the assignment he didn't consider whether or not he'd have to give the motor coach back. In the past he'd been able to keep items after he wrote the manual. However, he'd never worked on anything this large or expensive.

"I suppose I'll have to give it back," said Albert. He put his hand on the Venture. He realized he was actually going to miss it.

"Well maybe they'll let you buy it," said Sally. She looked at her watch. "I didn't realize it was so late," she said. "My shift ended a half hour ago."

"I'm sorry," said Albert.

"It's no problem," said Sally. "I was just wondering what I might do for dinner this evening."

"Albert," said the painting on the postcard from inside his pocket, "she wants you to invite her to dinner."

"I should probably think about eating too," said Albert.

"That's right," said Sally. "Except for Jack's chicken you've been eating peanut butter and jelly for two days."

"Yes," said Albert.

"Get on with it, Albert," said the painting. "Just ask her."

"I guess we'll be eating around the same time," said Albert.

"This is painful, Albert," said the painting. "It makes me want to...well, you know."

"The are a few good restaurants in town," said Sally.

"Maybe I could follow you to one of them," said Albert.

Sally laughed. "You'd have to unhook your water and electric."

"Oh," said Albert.

"Albert," scolded the painting.

"We could ride together," said Albert.

"That would be nice," said Sally. "Come on, we'll take my truck."

Sally drove them to a small place that specialized in wild fish caught in the nearby creeks. "Oh," she said as they began to look at the menu. "I should have asked if you like fish."

"I do," said Albert.

"Good," said Sally. "So where else have you been with the motor coach?"

"First I went to the bakery for bagels," said Albert. "Jacob makes very good bagels."

Sally laughed. "All trips start somewhere," she said.

Albert nodded. As they ate dinner, he told her about all of the other stops he'd made along the way. He talked about all of his nature walks, he described the dinosaur park and recounted his experience at the sculpture garden. Albert told her about Harvey and Edna and the way he'd played horseshoes and bocce.

"It sounds like you've had a full trip so far," she said.

"Yes," said Albert. "I've been thinking about this park, though. I wanted to see the waterfalls."

"They're beautiful," said Sally. "You're going to love it."

They finished their meal and Sally drove him back to the campsite. "Thank you for one of the nicest evenings I've had in a long time," said Sally as they were getting out the truck.

"Thank you," said Albert.

"You know," said Sally, "you're not like many of the other campers and tourists I meet around here."

"I've been told I'm not like most people," Albert admitted.

"That's a good thing," said Sally. "Here's my phone number. Just call if you need anything else – or if you want to talk."

"Give her your number," said the painting.

"I should give you my number," said Albert.

As he was telling her the number he heard another familiar voice. "Albert! There you are…we've been so worried about you." The statement was accompanied by the barking of several dogs.

Albert turned around to see Harvey coming towards him. He grabbed Albert by the shoulders with a combination of hugging and shaking. Edna came along with the dogs.

"After hearing you talk about the waterfalls, we decided to join you here," said Edna. "But the office said you'd never checked in to the campground."

"I got a bit lost," said Albert. "Sally's a ranger. She found me."

"More like he found me," said Sally.

"That's fantastic," said Harvey. "I'm so glad to see that you're safe." He clapped Albert on the shoulder. "Say Albert, have you ever played badminton?"

11

Albert always knew he'd appreciate seeing the waterfalls but his receipt experiences made seeing the waterfalls all the more special. He sat for a long time on a large rock watching the water cascading down several levels into a large misty pool.

Albert appreciated the beauty of the scene but he also enjoyed the serenity of the way the sound of the falls drowned out everything else. All he could hear was the sound of the water hitting the rocks and the pond below.

"I guess this is the real white noise," he said to himself. "I made it. I'm here."

The sound of the water was almost like applause. He was able to bask in that sound for awhile, but eventually his mind wandered.

"What next?" Albert asked himself. He could continue on to one of the other destinations. He could also return home. Albert had grown fond of traveling in the motor coach but he also missed his house. He missed cooking breakfast and dinner each day. He missed his weekly cleaning routine. He missed writing in his office.

Despite his mishaps with the bear and getting lost, Albert realized he was enjoying most of his time traveling. He enjoyed backing in the motor coach and setting everything up. He enjoyed taking nature walks and seeing new things. He enjoyed finding interesting places to stop along the road. Albert listened to the sound of the falling water. It only offered white noise; it did not offer advice.

"Who says I have to decide right now?" Albert asked himself. He stood up from the rock and made his way along the path to the front of the park. Albert scanned the surrounding forest several times. He certainly didn't want to run into any more bears…or undesirable choices.

12

Albert returned to the motor coach and sat down at the kitchen table. He took the old watch out of his pocket. "The time is one forty-two," it said. A pang of guilt rolled through him as he looked at the crack in the face.

"I will get you repaired," said Albert. "And I'll figure out where you belong."

"The time is one forty-three," said the watch. Albert took that as agreement. He put the watch back in his pocket.

"Welcome back, Albert," said the wallet. "Are you ready to go home now?"

"Let's pick another brochure," said the car keys. "This time we'll use the navigation system."

"It's good to hear you making at least some sense," said the wallet. "But I think Albert's had quite enough adventure for the time being."

"It was a couple of nights in the woods," said the car keys. "And he slept in the motor coach each night."

"Albert, that means you should appreciate your good fortune and not press your luck any further," said the wallet.

"Things did turn out okay," said the reading glasses. "And Albert learned some valuable lessons."

"And he can write about it in the manual," said the wallet. "Which, by the way, is almost finished."

"That just gives you more time to explore," said the car keys.

"That's true," agreed Albert.

"No," protested the wallet. "It means that you don't have a reason to be out here anymore."

"I've enjoyed the trip," said Albert.

"And what about Sally?" asked the cell phone. "If we leave here we might not get to see her again."

"Sally?" asked the wallet. "What does she have to do with anything?"

"She is my friend," said Albert.

"You've only known her for a couple of days," said the wallet. "I know she helped you out of the woods but that's no reason…"

"I found my own way out of the woods," said Albert.

"Regardless," said the wallet. "She is no reason to stay here."

"He would like to get to know her better," said the cell phone.

"He can always write to her," said the wallet. "It's not like he was ever going to be here permanently."

"Right," said the car keys. "There are too many other things to see."

"Albert isn't going to spend the rest of his days driving down the highway, either," concluded the wallet.

"What would be so bad about that?" asked the car keys.

"It might be difficult to make a living for one," said the wallet. "How would you get assignments, Albert?"

"I hadn't thought of that," said Albert. "Maybe I can write books about plants."

"Books about plants?" asked the wallet. "What are you talking about, Albert?"

"I was thinking that I'd like to write books about plants," said Albert.

"And how are you going to make money from that?" asked the wallet. "You've never sold a book. You make your living writing contracted instruction manuals."

"You can write manuals from anywhere," said the car keys. "You wrote most of this one from inside the motor coach."

"And you could always call the editor," said the cell phone.

"I could do that," said Albert.

"So it's settled," said the car keys. "Let's take a look at those brochures, Albert."

"You can look at the brochures all you want," said the wallet. "But it's time to go home."

"I haven't decided anything yet," said Albert. "I don't know whether I'm ready to go home."

"It's nice to have the choice," said the reading glasses.

"It is nice to have the choice," agreed Albert.

13

"Give it a try, Albert," said Harvey. "Don't worry about the bullseye. Just concentrate on hitting the board."

Albert drew back the dart and aimed at a dartboard hanging on a nearby tree. Harvey put it there so they could practice before the contest at the camp hall that night.

"I guess I'll give it a try," said Albert.

"Now that's the spirit," said the dart. "That's the great thing about you Yanks – you always have that 'can do' attitude."

Harvey gestured to the outer circle of the dartboard. "Just see if you can hit the outer ring here."

Albert tossed the dart at the board. It veered to the right and landed in the dirt. "Sorry," said Albert.

"No need to be sorry, old boy," said the dart. "Just a bit of grit is all."

"Try again," said Harvey.

Albert picked up the second dart and tossed it towards the board. He couldn't tell where that dart landed so he picked up the the third one.

"I say," said the third dart, "your friend appears to be bleeding quite a bit." Albert looked over to see that his previous dart hit Harvey square in the arm. It was sticking out by the tip and a trail of blood was running down to his hand.

"I'm really sorry," said Albert.

Harvey pulled the dart out of his arm and stuck it into the board. "Just a flesh wound," he said. "Maybe no more darts until after dinner, though."

Albert agreed and handed Harvey his third dart. They walked over to the picnic table and sat down. Edna was cooking hamburgers on a grill a few feet away.

"You're in for a treat, Albert. I can't believe you've never had a Gooey Louie before." Harvey explained that Gooey Louie was Edna's name for a burger with shredded cheese in the middle.

Sally joined them for dinner. After they finished eating Albert decided to ask them to take a look at the old watch. "I found this near my home," he explained. "I'm trying to find out more about it. Someone told me it was from around here."

"It is from around here," said Sally.

"You recognize it?" asked Albert.

"Not this watch specifically," said Sally. "But it looks like the type of watch the smokejumpers used to give the firefighters who come out here to help them."

"That could explain how it ended up out your way," said Harvey.

Sally nodded. "When the wildfires get bad," she explained, "firefighters from the east often come out here to help. Some of the guys around here like to give them a token of appreciation, especially if it's been a hard season."

"Is there any way to tell who might have given away that watch? Or who they gave it to?" asked Albert.

"Not for me," said Sally. "But there's a ranger a couple of counties over who's been dealing with wildfires for years. He might recognize it."

"Could be worth a try," said Harvey.

"You could drive it in about a day," said Sally. "And the facility there is nice. Full hookups, lots of trails. You probably already have information about it in your brochures."

Albert nodded. "I think I should talk to him," he said.

After helping Harvey and Edna clean up, Sally and Albert went back to the Venture so Sally could show him the way to the other ranger. As she predicted, Albert did have a brochure on the park. She marked the route on the map and wrote down the ranger's name and phone number.

"See," she said. "It's a fairly easy run...all highway."

"Can you come with me?" asked Albert.

"I'd like to," said Sally, "but I can't take off work right now. I'll call him to let him know you're on your way."

"Thank you again," said Albert.

"Don't mention it," said Sally. "Just make sure you stay in touch."

"I will," said Albert. "I could write to you."

Sally smiled at him. "That would be nice, Albert," she said. "No one writes anymore."

14

The next morning Albert was packing up the motor coach when he heard the cell phone. He recognized the number on the screen. It was his editor. He hadn't heard from the editor since he began the trip.

"How are you Albert?" asked the editor.

"I'm good," said Albert.

"Albert," proclaimed the editor, "I think that's the most confident I've ever heard you say that. Where are you?"

"I'm at a national park," Albert replied. "I've been traveling in the motor coach."

"I'm glad to hear that," said the editor. "I was a little worried you might just camp out in your driveway. How's the manual coming?"

"I'm almost finished," said Albert. "I have to proof it and there are a few inserts I need to write."

"That's good," said the editor. "The manufacturer has been extremely happy with the sections you've already sent over. However, they would like us to wrap it up in a couple of weeks. I still have to go through it more on my end, so that means I need it from you in a few days."

"I understand," said Albert.

"Also," continued the editor, "I know you usually get to keep the stuff you write about, but this case is a little different. They'd like the motor coach back. Even though it's technically used, they figure they can send it to shows and events as a sample."

"I understand," said Albert.

"Great," said the editor. "So you should probably start back for home if you aren't heading in that direction."

"Yes," said Albert. He realized he would be unable to visit the other ranger. "I was actually packing up when you called. I'll head home."

"Excellent," replied the editor. "I'm really looking forward to seeing this finished product. And I'm glad you decided to enjoy it."

"I did enjoy it," said Albert.

"I knew you would," said the editor. "Sometimes people just need a little nudge in the right direction. I'll see you soon, Albert."

"Yes," said Albert. He was about to let the editor hang up. "Wait…" he said. "I have a question."

"Sure," said the editor. "What is it?"

Albert considered how he might explain all this to the editor. "I found this watch a few weeks ago," he began. "I've been asking people about it and it turns out that someone nearby here might know more about it. I'm trying to return it to the original owner."

"Slow down, Albert," said the editor. "So you need to talk to someone out there about it?"

"Yes," said Albert. "But I have to drive to another park. It's about a day away. I won't be able to meet with the person if I have to go home now."

"Got it," said the editor. "So you need me to stall a bit."

"Yes," said Albert. "I just need a few days. Enough time to get to the other park and talk to the other ranger. Once I do that, I'll turn right around and head home."

"What about returning he watch?" asked the editor.

"It sounds like it belongs to someone near home," said Albert. "I just need to find out who that might be from the ranger."

"As long as you can wrap it up in three or four days," said the editor, "I can tell the manufacture we need a bit more time."

"Thank you," said Albert.

"Albert," said the editor, "in all the years we've worked together, this is the first time you've ever asked me for a favor. How can I refuse?"

"I appreciate it," said Albert.

"You're very welcome," said the editor. "If that's it, then…I have a meeting in about five minutes."

"Actually there's one more thing," said Albert. "I'd like to buy the motor coach."

The editor was quiet for a moment.

"I'm sorry," said Albert. "I didn't mean to presume…"

"It's not that at all," said the editor. "You just caught me by surprise. Let me see what I can do and I'll get back to you."

"Thank you," said Albert again.

"Albert…" said the editor.

"Yes," replied Albert.

"That must have been some trip you've been on," said the editor.

"I suppose it has been," said Albert.

15

"I'm sorry to see you go so soon Albert," said Harvey. "But we'll catch up with you at another park. I heard about this cornhole tournament in another campground…"

"I talked to my editor," said Albert. "They need me to finish up the manual. After I visit with the other ranger I need to head for home."

A look of disappointment came over Harvey's face. "So this is really goodbye, then?"

"Yes," said Albert. "The manufacturer also wants the motor coach back. I've offered to buy it but I don't know if they're going to sell it to me yet."

"I hope they do," said Harvey. "If not you should buy another one. You know, I have a buddy…"

"Don't you go trying to sell Albert that old wreck Jerry's been driving around," interjected Edna. She was back from walking the dogs. "You can do better than that old junk heap."

"That is a solid piece of machinery," disagreed Harvey.

"It's a solid piece of scrap metal you mean," said Edna. "It's been fun having you around, Albert. And I wish you good luck in your travels."

"Thank you," said Albert.

"And we hope to see you again," said Harvey. "You have our phone number now."

"Yes," said Albert.

"Have you told Sally?" asked Harvey.

"Not yet," said Albert. "I'm going to call her before I leave."

"I think I saw her in the south field," said Harvey. "Why don't you drive around and talk to her face to face."

"Well…" began Albert.

"Don't even finish that sentence," said Edna. "You go see her before you leave."

Albert nodded. He returned to the motor coach and made his final preparations to leave. This mainly consisted of spot checking everything to make sure it wasn't going to rattle around once he was on the road. After this was complete, he started the vehicle and drove through the campground and over to the south field.

He spotted Sally's truck and pulled up behind it. Albert got out of the motor coach and looked around. After a few moments he spotted Sally on a nearby hill. She waved and signaled she would come over.

"I called ahead for you," said Sally. "Ranger Marlow knows you're coming to talk to him."

"Thank you," said Albert.

"You're welcome," said Sally. "You didn't need to come down here just to say goodbye, though."

"I wanted to," said Albert. "After I meet with Ranger Marlow I have to return home. They're ready for me to turn in the manual…and the motor coach."

"Oh," said Sally. "So you're camping days are over?"

"At least for now," said Albert. "I offered to buy the motor coach but I won't know for awhile if that's possible. I hope I can."

"I hope so too," said Sally. "Travel suits you." She leaned over and kissed him on the cheek. Albert blushed. "Don't forget you promised to write," she said.

PART 5

1

For the first time since he'd begun this journey, Albert drove with a purpose. He remained focused on the road and barely took note of any scenery or attractions. He would meet with the ranger quickly and return home to finish the manual and return the motor coach.

"You are exceeding the recommended cruising speed for this vehicle," said the wallet.

"I need to get to Ranger Marlow," said Albert.

"If you are that worried about getting yourself or your editor in trouble," continued the wallet, "then you should return home now."

"If he doesn't talk to Marlow," said the cell phone, "he may never know anything about the watch."

"Is that really necessary?" asked the wallet. "All it ever says is the current time."

"It's a watch," said the car keys. "That's its job. Just like you only care about money and finances and just about anything that's completely boring."

"Sally went out of her way to make this introduction," said the reading glasses. "Ranger Marlow is expecting Albert."

"I wouldn't want to stand him up," said Albert. "He cleared part of his schedule to meet with me tomorrow."

"Again with Sally," said the wallet. "So much fuss over a person he's only known for a short time. And I'm sure Ranger Marlow has more important matters then talking about an old watch."

"The time is three forty-six," said the watch.

"See," said the wallet. "The watch knows it's place. It doesn't need any help from you, Albert."

"It knows it's purpose," said Albert. "Not necessarily it's place."

"Just because you happened to find it in a field," replied the wallet, "that doesn't make it your duty."

"I did break it," said Albert.

"So get if fixed," said the wallet.

"Albert, you have a turn coming up," announced the reading glasses.

"I see it," said Albert. "Thank you."

"You're welcome," said the reading glasses.

Albert took the next exit and merged onto a different highway. "It shouldn't be too long now," he said. "I'll get to the campground before dark and see Ranger Marlow first thing in the morning."

"And suppose he is able to tell you the owner of the watch," said the wallet. "What then?"

"That's just the start of another adventure," said the car keys.

"You'll be able to return the watch to the owner Albert," said the cell phone.

"And what if the owner lives far away?" asked the wallet.

"If that's the case," said Albert, "I suppose I'll have to go there after I've completed the manual."

"And if you don't have the motor coach anymore?" asked the wallet.

"I don't know," said Albert.

"There are hotels you know," said the car keys.

"Or you could travel with Harvey and Edna," suggested the cell phone.

"Oh please no," said the wallet.

"I have to agree with that sentiment," said the car keys.

Albert chuckled. "That might not be such a good idea," he said. "But I will try to find the owner, even if I have to wait until after the manual is finished."

"At least you're being sensible about that," said the wallet. "If you have to stay at a hotel you should really talk to the travel agent again."

"Yes," said the cell phone. "You can get help planning the trip."

"Or perhaps the owner will be close to home," said the reading glasses.

"Here's hoping, " said the wallet.

2

Albert entered the park office to find a ranger checking first aid kits. The ranger looked up at him. "Can I help you?" he asked.

"I'm looking for Ranger Marlow," said Albert.

"You must be Albert," said the ranger. "Go ahead and have a seat. I'm Marlow."

Albert sat down in a chair on the other side of the desk. "Thank you for seeing me today," he said.

"Just a moment," said Marlow. "I just need to finish this count." Marlow cataloged the last few first aid kits and then looked back at Albert. "So what can I help you with today?"

Albert took the watch out of his pocket and handed it to Marlow. "I found this watch back east and I've been trying to find the owner."

"And you think this might be a gift one of our rangers gave to a firefighter," finished Marlow.

"Yes,' said Albert. "Sally thought you might be able to help."

"Let me take a look at it," said Marlow. He looked at the watch for several minutes. He ran his fingers over the face and the back. His lips moved as he read the inscription over several times. He turned the winder. Then he held it to his ear.

"This is a very nice watch," Marlow concluded.

"Yes," said Albert. "I'm going to have the glass fixed."

"That should be easy enough,' said Marlow. "If the watch wasn't ticking, then you'd have a bigger problem. Does it keep good time?"

"Very much so," said Albert.

"Good," said Marlow. He continued to look at the watch for a moment, then stared out the window. Albert waited for the ranger to speak again. Eventually the ranger looked away from the window and back at Albert. He handed him the watch back.

"A very nice watch indeed," said Marlow.

Albert realized he might have to inquire further. "Do you recognize it?" he asked.

"Recognize that watch?" asked Marlow. Albert nodded. "I'm afraid I don't," Marlow replied.

"Do you think it was a gift to a firefighter who helped with the wildfires?" Albert inquired.

"That seems plausible," said Marlow. Then he resumed looking out the window.

"I was really hoping to find the watch owner," said Albert. "So that I could return it."

Marlow turned back from the window. "You seem like a nice enough fellow," he said, "and that's a noble intention but it doesn't seem very likely."

"If I could find out who gifted the watch…" Albert began.

"I don't see any way to help you do that," said Marlow. "We've had a number of wildfires over the years and each time we have volunteers. Many of the local firefighters and rangers have given volunteers watches as gifts. Some of the locals still work here but many are retired and a few have passed on."

"The inscription is very unique," said Albert.

"It is," said Marlow. "Did you try running a lost and found ad?"

"No," said Albert. "I hadn't thought of that."

"You could try that," said Marlow.

Albert slumped back in his chair. He looked down at the watch. "The time is eight thirty-four," said the watch. Albert put the watch back in his pocket.

"I'm sorry I wasn't able to offer you much information," said Marlow.

"I just thought…"Albert began. He got up from the chair and started to walk to the door.

"Look at it another way," said Marlow as Albert reached the doorway, "instead of finding the watch's former owner, maybe you should look for the person who should have it now."

Albert stopped at the doorway and considered this. "You think so?"

"Yes," said Marlow. "Or maybe just sell it online."

"Oh," said Albert. He started to go out the door.

"You could give the proceeds of the sale to charity," Marlow called after him.

Albert stopped to look back at Marlow. "I suppose I could do that," said Albert.

"Right," said Marlow. "Or just keep the money for yourself." Marlow began checking the first aid kits again as Albert left the office.

3

"Well that did not go as expected," said the car keys.

"That man was rather unhelpful," added the cell phone.

"Time to get on the road, Albert," said the wallet.

After speaking with the ranger, Albert had performed a few necessary chores in the motor coach and started on the road home. Ever since the call with his editor the vehicle was feeling less and less like it belonged to him. He wanted to get it back to the manufacturer in case they were unwilling or unable to sell it to him.

"Are you okay, Albert?" asked the reading glasses. "I know that wasn't the conclusion you expected."

"That wasn't a conclusion at all," said the car keys.

"It probably was a long shot from the start," said Albert. He watched as the trees and billboards rolled past the motor coach. Each billboard would start to talk but he had no time or desire to listen.

"Act now to…" began one. "Visit the best…" said another. "Ready to eat…" started the next. And so on and so on. Albert just wasn't interested.

"It's time that I get on with things," said Albert. "I'll get the motor coach back and put the finishing touches on the manual."

"You know Albert," said the wallet, "you may able to locate the watch's owner if you develop a good plan."

"What are you talking about?" asked the car keys.

"You can accomplish anything with a plan," said the wallet. "List out what you know and what you don't know. For the items you don't know, brainstorm some ways you can get answers."

"I don't know," said Albert.

"You've really only tried a few random ideas," said the wallet. "A more systematic approach would probably yield better results."

"You could certainly make more calls," said the cell phone.

"Right now I need to finish the manual," said Albert.

"I'm here to help if you should change your mind," said the wallet. "As long as you don't lock me in the closet again."

It was quiet in the motor coach for several moments. "That was a joke," the wallet added eventually.

"Are you developing a sense of humor?" asked the car keys.

"I always had a sense of humor," corrected the wallet. "It's just more selective than yours."

Albert began to relax as the hours and miles rolled by in the motor coach. He had enjoyed the trip but he felt good about heading home again.

"It seems like I'm going faster on the way back," concluded Albert.

"That's because there's no anticipation on the way back," explained the car keys.

"The time is five thirty-seven," called out the watch from its position on the dash.

"Dinner time," said Albert. He was starting to get hungry. "I'll go on a bit further and then stop for the night."

"The time is five thirty-eight," said the watch.

"Albert," said the cell phone, "have you considered the other advice the ranger gave you?"

"If I sold the watch," said Albert, "I wouldn't want to keep the money but I'm not sure where I would donate it."

"I'm talking about the other thing he said," explained the cell phone, "passing it on to someone else."

"Just give it to someone?" asked the car keys. "Who would he give it to?"

"Someone who would appreciate it," said the car keys.

"You want to give it to Harvey?" asked the car keys. "Or Edna? It would make an expensive chew toy for the dogs."

"What about Sally?" suggested the cell phone.

"He doesn't really know Sally that well," said the wallet. "A gift like that would be premature."

"Family campground….twelves miles ahead," announced one of the billboards. It was the first sign in many miles to catch Albert's attention.

"That should be a good place to stop for the night," said Albert. "It has a seal of approval I remember the travel agent showing me."

"You could go a little further," suggested the car keys. "I'm sure they'll be another campground within an hour or so of here."

"This is a good time to stop," said Albert. "I can eat and spend some time working on the manual."

"You should stop before you get too hungry or tired," agreed the reading glasses.

"And before it gets dark," added Albert.

4

Albert began the next day with a stop at a nearby gas station. He preferred to start the day on a full tank. Albert had studied his maps and knew that if he could get far enough today he could be home in under two days.

He pulled the motor coach beside the pump. While the tank was filling, he walked over to a vending machine by the side of the building.

Albert looked over his choices. "Maybe I'll have some nuts," he said.

"You don't want those nuts," interjected a package of cookies. "They've been in here for weeks. Look at the faded packaging."

"Why don't you mind your own business?" asked the nuts. "I'm nutritious. Besides, nuts don't go bad."

Albert thought about his. He wasn't sure if nuts went bad or not. He supposed they might go stale.

"I don't really want cookies, though," he said.

"Who doesn't want cookies?" replied the cookies. "You are a very strange man."

"Insulting the man isn't going to help," interjected a bag of pretzels.

"Thank you," said Albert.

"You're welcome," said the pretzels. "Now let me explain why pretzels are the perfect snack."

"I'm cutting back on my salt," said Albert.

"You are a very strange man," replied the pretzels.

"Buy a pack of gum," suggested a bag of chips sitting right the gum. "Gum is a great snack."

"I don't think gum is much of a snack," replied Albert.

"Look," explained the chips, "I've be behind this pack of gum for a month. No one buys gum from a vending machine. I need to get out of here."

Albert looked at the pack of gum. It was birthday cake flavor. He wondered why anyone would make a gum flavored like birthday cake.

"Who wants to chew on birthday cake for twenty minutes?" Albert commented.

"Hey," said the gum, "I didn't ask to get made."

Albert scanned each row of the machine. "I don't know what I feel like eating," he said.

"Popcorn," suggested a bag from one of the lower rows. "You feel like eating popcorn."

"The kernels will get stuck in your teeth," said a cinnamon bun on the first row. "Buy me. I'm huge."

Albert had to admit it was a large cinnamon bun. He decided that would be too sweet, though. "Maybe just cheese and crackers," he said.

"An excellent choice," said the package of cheese and crackers.

"Boring," said a brownie just above the cheese and crackers. "You want a brownie."

"I don't want anything sweet," said Albert.

"I'm not sweet and I can prove it," protested the brownie. "Your hair is a mess. You have poor choice in clothes. How's that for not sweet?"

"And they say I'm nuts," said the package of nuts.

Albert put his money into the machine and pressed the number for the cheese and crackers. The spiral spun several times, pushing on the package. The motion stopped just before the package dropped down into the slot.

"Uh oh," lamented the cheese and crackers. "This happened when someone bought the packaging in front of me."

"What now?" asked Albert.

"You have to call the number on the front of the machine," said the cookies. "This wouldn't have happened if you picked something heavier...like a nice package of cookies."

Albert tapped on the glass a couple of times. The package of cheese and crackers wobbled but did not drop. He gave the machine a little shake to no avail. Albert sighed and decided he wasn't all that hungry anyway.

As he walked away he could hear the package of crackers and cheese shouting "Help! Someone help me! I haven't fallen and I can't get down."

As Albert was finishing up at the pump, he noticed a familiar truck parked across from him. He was sure he'd seen it before but he couldn't place it. A moment later a person out of the gas station office. It was the woman he'd met at the sculpture garden.

"Ann?" asked Albert tentatively.

"Yes," replied the woman. A look of recognition flashed across her eyes. "Albert...from the sculpture park, right?"

Albert nodded and they shook hands. "I thought you would have gotten further than this by now," said Ann.

"I did," explained Albert. "I'm heading back home."

"Good trip?" asked Ann.

"It was," said Albert. "But it will be nice to be home again."

"I know how you feel," said Ann. "I spend a lot of time on the road and I'm always happy to get home."

"Yes," said Albert.

"Did you ever find out any more about that watch?" asked Ann.

"Not much," said Albert. "I spoke to a few people but no one could give me much information."

"That's too bad," said Ann. "It would have been nice to get it back to the owner."

Albert nodded. There was a flash of light in the distance followed by a distant rumbling. A thick row of dark clouds was forming along the horizon.

"Looks like we're going to get some weather," said Ann.

"I didn't see anything in the forecast," said Albert.

"These storms work up pretty quick sometimes," explained Ann. "Especially on this side of the mountains."

"I was planning a whole day of driving," said Albert. The two of them stood watching the storm gather for a few moments.

"You know," said Ann, "the next best thing is to have that watch be with someone who appreciates it. Maybe you should just keep it."

"I don't feel right just keeping it," said Albert.

"I know I already asked but do you want to sell it?" asked Ann. "I'll make sure it gets to someone who would treasure it – most likely wear it again."

Albert gave this some thought. He could sell the watch and then hold onto the money until he figured out where to donate it. Then he remembered the face was cracked.

"The face got cracked," said Albert. He was too embarrassed to explain the actual circumstances to Ann.

"Does it still work?" asked Ann.

"Yes," said Albert. "Still keeps perfect time."

As if to prove the fact to Albert the watch announced "The time is seven-twelve," from inside the cab of the motor coach.

"Glass is fixed easily enough," said Ann. "I could give you a hundred and twenty-five dollars for it."

Albert considered the offer but decided he wasn't ready to part with the watch yet. "Thank you," he said, "but I think I'd like to hold onto it for now."

"I understand," said Ann. "I'd better be getting back on the road. I have an appointment near here at seven thirty and I don't like to keep people waiting. Safe travels to you."

"You too," Albert replied. He watched Ann drive off before getting back into the motor coach.

"The time is seven fourteen," said the watch.

"So it is," said Albert. "So it is." In the distance he heard more thunder. This time it sounded much closer.

5

Albert only managed to drive about three hours before the storm became too much to manage. The howling winds and driving rain eliminated most of the visibility. Albert pulled the motor coach into a rest area and settled in to wait out the storm. Thanks to the generator he was able to have power.

Albert gathered up the last of his notes and revisions and began to compile the final version of the manual. He had finished all the sections and only need to make a few changes here and there. This was the largest project he'd ever created and he was nearing the end of it. Albert couldn't help looking at the nearly completed manuscript with pride.

"You've done an excellent job," said the reading glasses.

"This will really help people understand the motor coach," said the cell phone.

"I like that you've got in all the essentials," said the car keys.

"You've done a thorough job,' said the wallet.

Albert listened to the rain hitting the roof as he worked through the final changes. It was still raining several hours later as he finished. He leaned back in his chair and rubbed his eyes. "There it is," he announced.

"Excellent work," said the wallet.

"I have a good signal if you want to email it to your editor now," said the cell phone. Albert nodded and sent off the final document.

"So that's it then," said the car keys.

"I suppose that's it," Albert confirmed. He thought for sure he'd be tired at this moment but it was exactly the opposite. He felt invigorated and somewhat disappointed that there was nothing more to write for the project.

"What do I do now?" asked Albert.

"You could just relax," said the reading glasses.

Albert looked at the watch. "The time is seven thirty-six," it said.

"Too early to go to bed," said Albert.

"Start writing something else then," suggested the car keys. "Since you're cooped up in here anyway."

Albert looked down at the blank screen in front of him. "I don't know what to write," he said.

"You should really plan it out anyway," said the wallet. "Why don't you compile a list of potential topics and then you can examine the pros and cons of each one."

"That's not writing," said the car keys. "That's analyzing."

"And it sounds boring," added the car keys.

"Have you ever thought of writing anything else?" asked the reading glasses.

Albert rubbed his chin and thought about this. He remembered his nature walks. "I could write a book about plants," he said.

"Plants again?" came the collective response.

"What would you write about plants?" asked the car keys.

"Different kinds of plants," Albert replied tentatively.

"What kind of plants exactly?" asked the wallet.

"All kinds?" asked Albert.

"There are a lot of books about plants," said the wallet. "You currently have eleven on your bookshelf at home."

"You seriously know how many books about plants he owns?" asked the car keys.

"Of course,' said the wallet. "Would you like to know how much he paid for each one?"

"I'll pass," said the car keys. "But I see the point. What would be unique about your book?"

"I don't know," said Albert. "Maybe I could focus on nature walks. That's the way I came up with the idea."

"Albert," inquired the wallet, "Do you want to write a book about plants or do you just want to write a book?

Albert considered this for several minutes. "I just want to write a book," he said.

"Which brings us back to the original question," said the car keys. "What would you write a book about?"

"I don't know," said Albert.

"You should probably write about something you enjoy," said the reading glasses.

"Or you could write a story," suggested the cell phone.

Albert thought about this option for awhile. "What story would I tell?" he asked.

"Tell the story about your brother," suggested the reading glasses.

"That's not a good story," said Albert.

"I agree," the postcard of the painting called out from it's position on the refrigerator. "His brother is not a likable character."

"What would you know about likable characters?" asked the cell phone. "You've been in a silent yell for a hundred years. No one even knows why you're upset."

"I illuminate the human condition," replied the postcard.

"What human condition?" asked the car keys.

"THE human condition," replied the postcard. "I don't think people want to hear the story of your brother."

"That's because you've never heard the story," said the cell phone.

"I don't want to tell that story," said Albert.

"You never talk about it," said the cell phone. "Even with your brother."

"We don't talk about that day at the beach," said Albert. "I can write about something else."

"Like plants?" asked the car keys.

"Like how to do things," said Albert. "Maybe how to do them for the first time."

"Like what?" asked the wallet.

"Well…" began Albert, "camping or travel for one thing. I just did it for the first time."

"I suppose I can't argue with that," said the wallet.

"I write about how to do things all the time," said Albert. "Usually just one thing at a time."

6

The rain did not let up until early afternoon the following day. By that time, Albert had outlined several ideas for potential books and sent them to his editor.

He decided to play a hand or two of solitaire while he waited for a reply.

"Don't put me there," protested a black seven. "You have a red a eight right over there." Albert signed and placed the black seven on the red eight and started to flip over a card from the pile.

"Hello," called out a red four he recently uncovered. "Put me over there on the black five." Albert sighed again and moved the card over. Then he turned over the card underneath. It was a red king.

"I suppose I'm going to be a problem for you," the king said rather smugly. "There are three more cards underneath me."

"Just throw him back into the pile," said a black two.

"That's cheating," protested the king.

"It's solitaire," replied the two card. "Everyone cheats."

Albert shook his head and counted out three cards from the pile, turning over the third. It was the "rules for pinnacle" card.

"No wonder you're in such a predicament," said the king. "You didn't even prepare the cards properly. I bet you didn't remove the jokers either." Albert had to admit he had forgotten to remove the jokers from the deck as well.

"All the more reason to just put his majesty at the bottom of the pile," suggested the black two.

"Yes," agreed a jack in another pile. "No one likes him and his mocking little smile anyway."

"Off with his head," announced a red queen underneath the jack.

The other cards began to chime in…"To the back of the pile!"

"Discard him!" shouted others.

Before he knew it, Albert was caught up in a coup. He glanced around the room before quickly grabbing the king and placing it at the bottom of the pile. The other cards all let a cheer in unison.

"Long live the king," said the black two sarcastically.

"Long live the king," replied Albert as he continued with the game.

The cell phone began to ring. It was his editor. Albert took a deep breath and answered the phone.

"I got your final version of the manual last night," said the editor. "Everything looks good. Are you still on the road?"

"Yes," said Albert. "I'm on my way back, but I ran into a storm. I'm waiting it out now."

"The main thing is for you to get home safe Albert," replied his editor. "And I spoke them about you buying the motor coach. They were planning to use that unit as a demonstration model but they're going to see if they can work things out."

"Thank you," said Albert.

"At the very least, they said you can have one of the first ones off the line once they've cleared up some existing orders," said the editor. "Probably four to six months."

"I'd really like to keep this one if possible," said Albert. "I'm comfortable with it."

"I understand Albert," said the editor. "I'll keep working on it."

"I appreciate it," said Albert.

"So let's talk about the other file you sent me," said the editor.

"Yes," said Albert. He held his breath.

"I like the ideas a lot Albert," said the editor. "And you're definitely well qualified to write this kind of book."

Albert had the feeling there was a large "but" coming his way.

"But our company doesn't really handle that kind of thing," said the editor.

Albert's heart sank. "I understand," he said.

"Let me finish,' said the editor. "I've wanted to take on a project like this for awhile. I'd like to work with you directly and see where we can take this. In the meantime, we'll keep giving you assignments for manuals."

"I appreciate that," said Albert. "I wasn't sure if you would like the ideas."

"I'm happy to do it," said the editor. "I don't know anyone who knows more about things than you do, Albert."

The rain let up as they talked and Albert knew it was time to get back on the road. The editor wished him safe travels and they agreed to speak once Albert had returned home.

Albert prepared the motor coach for travel again. He packed up his workplace and locked the drawers and cabinets. He went to the refrigerator to get some water to keep with him in the cab.

"That seemed to go well," said the painting on the postcard.

"Yes," said Albert.

"I'm glad for you Albert," said the postcard.

"Thank you," said Albert.

"I've changed my mind about the other idea, though," said the postcard.

"What's that?" asked Albert.

"It sounds like you need to talk to your brother," said the postcard.

"I'll probably meet him for lunch after I get home," replied Albert.

"I mean really talk to him," said the postcard. "I don't know the story, but it sounds like something you should talk about."

"We don't talk about that day," said Albert. "It was all my fault and I accept that."

"What was your fault?" asked the postcard.

"The whole thing," said Albert. He returned to the cab of the motor coach.

"I'm just trying to illuminate the human condition," the postcard called after him.

7

A warm feeling began to grow inside of Albert as he travelled roads he knew well and passed scenery he recognized from his daily routines. He was almost home again.

"Home stretch," said the reading glasses.

"Yes," agreed Albert.

He completed the final miles of his journey and turned the corner onto his own street. He almost pulled directly into the driveway but stopped short of it. Albert positioned the motor coach in the center of the road and backed into the driveway without an issue.

"Just like a pro," said the car keys.

"A fortuitous end," said the wallet.

"Welcome home," said the cell phone.

Albert let out a deep breath and turned off the engine. He patted the wheel and got out of the vehicle. Albert made his way to the front door, unlocked it and went inside. The air in the house was overly warm and a bit tight. That didn't stop Albert from taking a deep breath as he rested his hand on the frame of the front door.

However, he did go directly to the thermostat and lower the temperature to get the air flowing into the house again. He thought about opening the windows but decided it was too hot outside.

"The air will be faster," he concluded.

"Albert?" a voice called from the kitchen. "Is that you?" It was the oven.

"He's home," announced the microwave.

Albert nodded to a flurry of greetings as he walked down the hallway into the living room and flopped down on the couch. He rested for a few moments before heading back out to the motor coach to unpack.

Just as the journey outward seemed to take longer than the journey back, moving everything out of the motor coach took much less time. Albert emptied the

Venture in only a couple of hours. He then gave the motor coach a thorough cleaning.

Back inside the house, Albert made a simple dinner of soup and a sandwich using some leftover food from the trip. He watched a baseball game on television as he ate.

Afterward, Albert went through the house making sure everything was clean and in working. Then he sat back down on the coach in the living room. The baseball game was still on the television, so he watched the end of the game while retracing his route on the map.

Once the game was over he turned off the television and went upstairs to bed. Albert was extremely tired from the drive and from unpacking. Still, he found it difficult to sleep. He was too busy replaying different scenes from the trip in his head. Albert recalled his early troubles parking the motor coach. He remembered playing horseshoes with Harvey. He thought about his strolls through the sculpture garden.

Albert even spent time thinking about those nights he was lost in the woods. It made him appreciate the fact that was he was safe at home, lying in his own bed. There were times he couldn't even envision a way out.

He finally drifted off to sleep simply thinking about traveling down the road. He imagined the rows of trees passing by on either side of him, broken up only by billboards announcing the attractions at upcoming exits. Albert found himself driving the motor coach in many of his dreams that night.

Then he fell into a deep sleep. Albert slept better than he had in a long time. Not even the car alarm down the street woke him up.

8

Albert listened as the phone rang several times. He was about to give up and hang up when he heard the voice on the other end.

"Hello?" asked Sally.

"Hello," replied Albert. "It's me…Albert."

"Well hello stranger," replied Sally. "How are you? Did you get caught in that row of storms that came across?"

"Yes," said Albert. "I got home yesterday."

"Glad to hear it," said Sally. "I thought you were going to write, though."

"I'm sorry," said Albert. "You wanted to know when I got home safe and I thought the call would be faster."

"Relax," said Sally. "I'm just kidding with you. So how does it feel to be home?"

"Very comfortable," said Albert.

"That's good," said Sally. "Did you finish your work?"

"Yes," said Albert. "I was able to finish up while I was waiting out the rain."

"Good for you," said Sally. "Did you hear if you'll be able to buy the motor coach?"

"Not yet," said Albert. "They were planning to use it for shows."

"You can always buy another one," said Sally. "I know a couple of dealers that might be able to help you."

Thinking about that made Albert realize just how accustomed he'd become to the Venture. He didn't really want another motor coach. At least he couldn't imagine himself traveling in another one.

He must have been quiet for awhile because Sally restarted the conversation. "Still with me?" she asked.

"Yes," said Albert. "Just thinking."

"Nothing wrong with that," said Sally. "I meet a lot of people who never think. Did you decide what you're going to do with the watch?"

"Not yet," said Albert. "I do think I'm going to get the face repaired."

"It is a nice watch," said Sally.

"That's what people keep saying," said Albert.

"Well they're right," said Sally.

They spoke for several more minutes, although Sally did most of the talking. She told Albert about a bear they needed to capture and move further away from the campsites.

"They almost get tame," explained Sally. "People leave too much food out. One of these days someone is going to get hurt."

"People should be much more careful," agreed Albert, recalling his own encounter with the bear."

"Yes," said Sally. "Look at the time. I'm sorry Albert. I have to leave for my shift."

"I'm sorry," said Albert. "I hope I didn't make you late."

"I'll be fine Albert," said Sally. "You take care."

"You too," said Albert.

"And you better keep that promise to write to me," said Sally. "Especially since you're a professional writer."

This made Albert realize he'd forgotten to tell her about his book ideas. He didn't want to keep her so it would have to wait for now. Albert decided it would make a good topic for his first letter.

Albert put down the phone. "I suppose I should do some cleaning," he said.

"You cleaned last night when you got home," said the cell phone. "I believe you have another call to make."

"I should run some errands," Albert replied. "I have almost no food in the house."

"You said earlier you were eating out tonight," replied the cell phone. "It's meatloaf night at the diner. That's your favorite."

"I'll get ready for dinner then," said Albert.

"It's just after three," said the cell phone.

"The time is six after three," said the watch from its position on the table.

"You should make your other call," said the cell phone.

"I can do that tomorrow," said Albert. "He's probably busy right now."

"He's likely to be busy any time," said the cell phone. "Just call your brother and let him know you're back home safe."

Albert sighed and picked the phone back up. He dialed his brother's number. His brother picked up almost immediately.

"Albert!" he said. "Is that you?"

"Yes," said Albert.

"Thank God," said his brother. "I saw your number on the caller ID, but I was worried it was going to be a policeman or park ranger or something."

"Just me," said Albert.

"Where are you?" asked his brother.

"I'm home," said Albert. "I finished my trip and the manual for the motor coach."

"And you're not injured?" asked his brother.

"No," said Albert. "I did get lost in the woods at one point, but I found my way back out."

"I'm glad to hear your voice Albert," said his brother. "I was very worried about you."

"Everything was fine," said Albert.

"Except for getting lost," said his brother. Albert suddenly regretted even mentioning that he had gotten lost.

"That's just it," said Albert. "Even that worked out okay."

"When I think of everything that could have gone wrong," said his brother.

"But it didn't," protested Albert.

"You could have run out of gas…" said his brother.

"I did run out of gas," said Albert.

"You could have run into a bear…" said his brother.

"I did," said Albert. "And it was still okay."

His brother didn't seem to hear him and continued to list potential dangers. They spoke for several more minutes without really saying anything. Finally, Albert and his brother decided to meet for lunch in a couple of days.

"I'm half expecting you to be on crunches when I see you," said his brother.

"No crutches," said Albert. "Maybe a few more gray hairs."

"I know I have several more," replied his brother.

9

"Wake up Albert," announced the alarm clock with its familiar buzz. Now that he was home Albert had gotten back in the habit of waking up at a regular time each morning.

After his morning routine, Albert walked to the end of the driveway and opened the door of the mailbox. A fairly substantial pile of mail awaited him inside.

"I wouldn't get too excited," cautioned the mailbox. "It's all bills and junk mail."

Albert pulled out the mail out and began to flip through it. The mailbox was correct. The first two envelops were the electric bill and the cable bill. The next one announced that he was pre-approved and encouraged him to take advantage of this limited time offer.

"Keep going," said the mailbox. "It gets better."

The next letter appeared to be from a car manufacturer. Albert opened it quickly, worried it might be a recall of his car. It turned out that a local dealer wanted to buy back a car Albert had traded in a couple of years ago. It pleaded with him that his model was in high demand and must be bought back from him.

"That's not what they told me two years ago," said Albert.

"I warned you," said the mailbox.

Albert quickly flipped through the remaining mail. He found two more letters soliciting him to buy something or take out a loan and several store circulars. He separated out the bills and made a pile out of the rest.

"You should put a recycle can right underneath me," suggested the mailbox. "And save yourself a trip."

"That's not a bad idea," said Albert.

"It didn't use to be like this, you know," said the mailbox, which was old and had been there as long as the house. "Back in the day all sorts of important things came in the mail. There would be cards and letters…and not just at Christmas."

"Uh huh," said Albert. He was looking over his cable bill. It seemed to have gone up again.

"Paychecks and other important information," the mailbox continued. "And after people read the mail they'd write their own letters. They'd put a stamp on it and leave it here. They'd put that little flag up to let the mailman know there was something inside."

"Yes," said Albert absentmindedly. "I don't remember signing up for this subscription."

"Are you listening to me?" asked the mailbox.

"Of course," said Albert.

"I don't think you are," said the mailbox. "It's been years since anyone has put up the little flag."

Albert suddenly felt bad for the mailbox. "I don't get a lot of mail," said Albert. "It's always just bills or letters addressed to the occupant."

"Exactly," agreed the mailbox. "We are so misunderstood."

"Yes," said Albert. He tried to remember the last time someone sent him a card or letter. His brother an few other relatives sent him cards at Christmas.

"You're probably going to pay those bills online," said the mailbox.

"I was," admitted Albert. He'd gotten into the habit of paying the bills online during the trip. It was easier while he was away.

"See," said the mailbox. "No letters, no flag."

Albert thought about this. He decided he would make it a point to send something by mail soon. He would put it in the mailbox and raise the little red flag.

The final piece of mail was a packet from his editor. He had sent him a new manual assignment. Albert was also working on a travel guide for people starting out later in life.

"Make sure you put in your experiences," said his editor. "Write about your trouble backing up coming across the bear. Those stories are going to set your book apart."

As Albert started to look through the new assignment, another delivery service brought him a package. Inside was the device for his new assignment.

Albert was anxious to work on the book but decided to start on the new assignment first. He took the device out of its packing and set it on his desk. Albert took a long look at each side, running his fingers over the buttons. Then he plugged in the device. It emitted three beeps and the display and buttons flashed several times.

"What exactly is that contraption?" asked the postcard of the painting. Albert had pinned it to the bulletin board above his desk.

"I'm a multi-function cooker," announced the device proudly. "I am capable of producing a complete meal in as little as twenty minutes in express mode. And my slow cooking mode provides rich flavors…"

"I'm sorry I asked," said the painting.

Albert began typing as the device continued, "To get started," it explained, "choose a mode based on the primary protein, type of dish or overall cooking time."

Albert pressed one of the buttons. The device emitted a loud beep and the display and buttons began to flash again.

"That is the reset button," said the device. "It is not one of the mode buttons."

"Sorry," said Albert. He leaned towards the screen of his computer and re-read his last sentence.

"You seem distracted today Albert," said the reading glasses.

"You should start the travel book," the car keys called out from a hook on the wall.

"The new manual has priority," said the wallet. "Even the editor mentioned that."

"I wasn't thinking about the travel book," said Albert.

"Is it Sally?" asked the cell phone expectantly.

"No," Albert replied. He wheeled his desk chair over to the bookcase and pulled out a photo of two young boys off the shelf.

"Your brother," said the cell phone.

Albert nodded. "I couldn't help him then and I can't seem to help now."

"Help him with what?" asked the painting.

"Just help him," said Albert.

He looked at the photo again. In it, he and his brother were standing in front of the family car. Looking closer, Albert could see his brother's inflatable raft in one of the windows.

"My father took this just before we left for that trip," said Albert.

"What happened?" asked the painting. "Was it worse than being lost in the woods?"

Albert considered this. He had shelter, food and water while he was in the woods. His brother had none of those things. He put the picture face down on the desk.

"The raft told me he was getting too far out. I didn't listen," said Albert.

"Where were you?" asked the painting.

"I was at the edge of water," said Albert. "Each time the water would rush back out, there would be all of these tiny clams at the edge of the sand. I kept watching them bury their way back down."

"It sounds like you were distracted," said the painting.

"I was angry," said Albert. "I wanted to go out in the raft. My brother wouldn't let me. He said there wasn't enough room, but it was a two person raft."

"You had every right to be angry," said the car keys.

"Your brother was older," said the reading glasses. "He might have been worried about you."

"I don't understand what he was doing out there," said the wallet. "It seems like it was a bad idea from the start."

"He wanted to look for fish," said Albert. "He couldn't see anything through the waves, so he kept moving further out. The raft got caught in the current and it was too hard for him to paddle back. I stood and watched as he drifted further and further away."

"How long was he out there?" asked the painting.

"He had drifted almost twenty miles. Any longer and he would have been lost at sea," Albert replied. "He was so small in the middle of all of that water. The Coast Guard found him the next morning."

"He must have been scared," said the painting.

"Yes," said Albert. "When they found him he was dehydrated and severely sunburnt. He still has the scars."

"I'm sorry Albert," said the painting. "I guess I'm not always that good at illuminating the human condition."

"It was my fault," said Albert. "I was there when he was drifting out. I didn't do anything. I didn't tell anyone. I would look up at him every so often, but I mostly kept watching those little clams."

Albert picked up the photo of he and his brother and stared at for a moment before putting it back on the bookshelf. He rolled back to the desk and stared at the mostly blank screen on his computer.

"In case you we're wondering," said the cooking device, "I could have fully cooked a frozen chicken during this time."

10

The smells of pot roast filled Albert's house. In the kitchen, the new device was cooking a mixture of meat, potatoes and carrots in a rich broth. Albert was sitting at the table typing on the computer. He'd finished the manual for the cooker fairly quickly.

"I guess once you document an entire motor coach," observed the car keys, "a slow cooker isn't such a big deal."

"He still has a lot of proofreading to do," said the wallet. "Nonetheless, you've done a very good job on this one."

"I'll starting proofing tomorrow," said Albert. "It's always good to let a document sit for awhile." He got up from his chair and went over to the counter to check on the cooking device. He opened one of the counter drawers and took out a wooden spoon.

"Excuse me," interrupted the cooking device. "There's no stirring necessary. And if you take off the lid you'll only reduce the temperature."

"I was going to taste…" Albert began.

"It is unsafe to consume meat before it has fully reached a safe temperature" said the cooking device.

"Excellent advice," said the wallet. "I knew I liked this new appliance."

Albert put the wooden spoon back in the drawer. Looking up, he saw the motor coach sitting in the driveway outside the kitchen window. Albert hadn't heard anything about it from the editor and he didn't want to press the issue. He also did not want to become any further attached to the vehicle before he knew whether or not he'd be able to keep it. Albert left the counter and sat back down at the table.

"What are you going to do until dinner?" asked the car keys. "Maybe you should go for a drive."

"I am capable of cooking a meal without any intervention," said the cooking device.

"No ones likes a show off," said the oven.

"I agree," said the microwave.

"Why don't you write a letter to Sally?" suggested the cell phone.

"I like that idea," said the reading glasses.

Albert also thought it was a good idea. He started to type a greeting on his computer and stopped. He got up from the table and went over to another drawer in the kitchen. After rummaging around he managed to find some writing paper and a pen. Albert sat back down at the table and restarted the letter.

"Dear Sally…" he began. "I hope all is well with you. Everything is good here." At this point, Albert began to tap his pencil on the table.

"What's the matter Albert?" asked the cell phone.

"Isn't it obvious," replied the wallet. "He has no idea what to say next. It's not your fault, Albert. You barely know this woman."

"Letters are a good way to get to know someone," said the reading glasses.

"Yes," said the cell phone. "Ask her something about herself."

"I did," said Albert. "I asked her how things were."

"No," pointed out the wallet. "You said you hoped everything was already well with her."

"Oh," said Albert.

"That's okay," said the car keys. "Just talk about yourself."

"He can't just talk about himself," said the cell phone.

"Why not?" asked the car keys. "At least it's a topic that he knows about."

"I suppose you could talk about the things you've been doing since you got home," suggested the reading glasses.

"It's a start," said Albert. He wrote about starting work on the new manual and the travel book.

"Now ask about her," said the cell phone.

"Or tell her you enjoyed the trip," said the reading glasses. "Talk about your favorite parts."

"That's not bad," said Albert. He wrote about his favorite parts of the trip including playing bocce and walking through the sculpture garden."

"Now ask about her," suggested the cell phone again.

"All right," said Albert. He asked about how her season was going and how she made out with the bear near the campsites.

"What next?" asked Albert.

"I think that's it," said the car keys.

"I agree," said the reading glasses. "It's a good first letter."

"Yes," said Albert.

He signed his name at the bottom and placed the letter in an envelop. Albert searched the kitchen drawers for a stamp. He eventually found one stuck to a menu from a Chinese restaurant. Albert slowly and carefully pulled it off the menu and then placed on the envelop.

Albert looked at the old watch. "The time is four forty-seven," it said.

"If I take the letter now," he said, "It will go out today."

"An excellence plan," said the cell phone.

"I wouldn't exactly call it a plan," said the wallet. "But it's a good idea."

Albert walked down to his mailbox placed the letter inside of it. He made a point to raise the little red flag. As he walked back up to the house, Albert wondered whether or not he'd written the right things.

"The letter itself is the important thing," he concluded.

"That's what I've been saying for years," the mailbox called out from behind him. Albert looked back and gave it a nod before heading back inside.

The house smelled even more like pot roast. "Your meal is now complete," called out the cooking device. "You may now remove the lid and enjoy."

11

"I haven't seen you for awhile," said the hostess at the restaurant as she walked Albert to his usual table.

"I was traveling," Albert said proudly.

"Good for you," said the hostess. "I'll bring the other gentleman over to your table when he arrives. Enjoy your meal."

"Thank you," said Albert. He looked up at the painting of the Scream across from the table.

"Hello Albert," said the painting. "I hope it goes well today."

"It's just the human condition," said Albert.

"I would laugh if I wasn't screaming," said the painting.

Albert's brother entered the restaurant and sat down across from him. "Hello Albert," he said.

"Hello," Albert replied.

Albert's brother picked up the menu and began to study it. The pair sat in silence for several minutes. Eventually the waitress took their order. After she left Albert's brother began to re-arrange his silverware.

Albert finally broke the silence, "I started a new manual," he said.

"Please tell me it's not another recreational vehicle," replied his brother.

"No," said Albert. "It's a slow cooker. I'm almost finished actually. How is your work?"

"It's fine," said his brother.

"How is your new assignment going?" asked Albert.

"I'm not working on that project anymore," replied his brother.

"It's finished?" asked Albert.

"No Albert," said his brother. "It's not finished. Apparently they felt another manager could do it better."

"I'm sorry," said Albert.

"It's fine," said his brother.

Albert stared down at his plate. "I'm sorry," he said again.

"I said it's fine, Albert. There's no need for you to be sorry. It's not your fault," said his brother.

"I mean I'm sorry about that day," said Albert.

"What day?" asked his brother. He stopped fiddling with his silverware and napkin. "What are you talking about?"

"That day at the beach," said Albert. "When I didn't help you."

"I don't like to talk about that day," said his brother. He rubbed the scar on his face.

"Neither do I," said Albert. "But I've never apologized to you. I saw you were drifting out but I didn't help you."

Albert's brother leaned closer to him. "Albert you were only six. I was barely ten. There wasn't much you could do about it."

"But I didn't do anything," protested Albert. "I didn't try to help you. I didn't tell anyone."

"Albert," said his brother, "is that what you think? That my…getting lost…was your fault?"

"It was," said Albert. "I could have stopped it."

"You weren't a good swimmer Albert," said his brother. "That's why I didn't want you on the raft in the first place. Dad and Mom weren't around. They were having trouble with the car, remember? They left us to play on the beach while they tried to fix it."

"I should have gone to get them," said Albert.

"Is that what you've thought all these years?" asked his brother. "That I blamed you for that day?"

"It was my fault," said Albert.

"Look at me," said his brother. He gestured towards his eyes. The pair made solid eye contact for the first time in years. "That day was not your fault. And I've never blamed you for it."

"But you're always…" Albert began.

"Albert, that day changed me," explained his brother. "It showed me the risk in life. All I wanted to do was look at some fish and I ended up almost dying in a twenty dollar raft."

"I know," said Albert. "If I had done something…"

"There was nothing you could do," said his brother. "You were just a kid. I was just glad it was only me on the raft. When I was floating out there alone, the one thought that gave me relief and comfort was that I didn't let you on the raft that day."

"I was mad at you," said Albert. "Because you wouldn't let me on the raft."

"I know you were," said his brother. "And I know you don't like it whenever I warn you not to do something. But I only want to protect you. Life is full of risks, but you can avoid most of them if you just make careful choices."

"I know you're just trying to help me," said Albert. "Do you ever wonder if we're missing out though?"

"Every day Albert," replied his brother. "Then I think about you and my wife and my children and I know that we're all safe…at least until you go driving off in a motor coach and get lost in the woods and attacked by bears and bocces."

"Bocce is just a game," said Albert.

"Whatever," said his brother. "When you're at home writing about coffee makers at least I know you're safe."

"I was really worried all of those times," said Albert. "Even the first time I played bocce. But I got through all of it. I wasn't attacked by the bear and I found my way out of the woods. Just like you survived on the raft."

"We were both lucky," said his brother.

Albert considered this. He couldn't deny that he had experienced some luck. The bear eventually walked away and left him alone. He stumbled out on the road not far from the general store with a park ranger inside.

Then he realized that he also made good choices. He knew not to run from the bear. He figured out that he was in the fire break. He followed the creek until he was out of the woods.

"And you knew not to drink the water," he said out loud to his brother.

"Well of course not,' said his brother. "That's why I was so dehydrated the next day. If I drank the salt water it may have killed me."

"We were both in danger," said Albert, "but we knew to make the right choices."

Albert waited for a reply but his brother was silent. By this time, the waitress had brought their food so they spent most of the time eating quietly.

"I suppose that conversation is over," said the painting. "He is a tough one."

They finished their meal and his brother signaled for the check. Albert worried his brother was not going to speak again. This was the first time they had ever discussed the day at the beach. Albert felt better about it. His brother seemed only troubled by the conversation.

Albert was unsure what to do next. He looked up at the painting but it offered no advice. It stood frozen in its perpetual pose, appearing to express only anxiety and fear about Albert's relationship with his brother.

Then he heard a voice from his pocket. "The time is one-fourteen," it said. Albert felt around in his pocket and took out the watch. His brother was busy calculating the tip for the waitress.

Albert turned it over and looked and the inscription. "For TM. Much appreciation and good fortune." He turned it back over and looked at the cracked face. Then he looked at his brother.

"Here," Albert said. "I want you to have this. He slid the watch over to his brother.

His brother looked up from the bill. "What Albert?"

"I found this watch some time ago," said Albert. "I got it working again. The face is cracked, but I want you to have it."

Albert's brother took the watch in his hand and looked at it. He ran his thumb over the crack in the face and then turned it over. He read the inscription several times.

"This inscription is for someone else," said his brother.

"I couldn't find the owner," said Albert. "But sometimes it's not about finding the original owner. It's about finding the right owner."

12

Albert was in the middle of his usual cleaning routine when the cell phone began to ring. He answered and was greeted by his editor.

"Excellent work on the slow cooker," said the editor. "Not that I expected any different."

"You're welcome," replied Albert. "It actually cooks very well. I've made several meals in it already. I think my stove is jealous."

The editor laughed. "Albert I think that may be the first time I've ever heard you make a joke."

"I was being serious," said Albert.

The editor laughed again. "The travel book also looks great so far...a good balance of information and personal experience."

"Thank you," said Albert. "Did you talk to your publishing contacts?"

"I did," replied the editor. "That's the bad news. They're not really interested in anything unsolicited. It turns out very few publishers want to work with unpublished authors."

"Then how does anyone get published?" asked Albert.

"That's what I keep trying to figure out," said the editor. "It doesn't matter, though. We're going to publish it on our own."

"How?" asked Albert.

"You're a writer and I'm an editor," the editor replied. "We certainly know how to put a book together. And there are companies that will publish it for us."

"But how do we sell it?" asked Albert.

"We market it," replied the editor. "Even if we did sign with a major publisher, we'd still end up doing our publicity and marketing."

"Oh," said Albert.

"Listen," explained the editor, "you do the writing and I'll worry about the rest. And in the meantime we have plenty of manual writing to pay the bills."

"All right," said Albert.

"Now about that giant vehicle sitting in your driveway," continued the editor.

"Yes?" asked Albert.

"I finally heard back from the manufacturer. Another customer has agreed to allow them to use his unit as the demonstration model in exchange for a discount. That means you can buy the one you have."

"Really?" asked Albert.

"Yes," said the editor. "And you're getting a great discount. They're selling it to you at cost and they'll even finance it for you."

"So I can keep it?" asked Albert.

"The manufacturer will send you the paperwork directly," replied the editor. "You should have it in a couple of days."

They spoke for a few more minutes before the editor had to take another call. Albert was a bit worried about the idea of them publishing the travel book on their own. He didn't dwell on it much though. He was too excited to learn that he would be able to purchase the Venture. Now that he knew he'd be able to keep it, he went back inside for the first time.

Albert gathered up many of the tools, equipment and other items he'd removed and put them back into the motor coach. He made the bed back up with fresh sheets and put the hoses into the outside storage compartments. He loaded the kitchen cabinets with cups, plates and silverware.

"Are you going on another trip?" asked the car keys expectantly.

"Not now," said Albert. "Soon enough."

"Soon enough," repeated the car keys. "What does that even mean? You can say either 'I'm leaving soon' or 'I've had enough' but you can't say both."

"I think it's just an expression," said the cell phone.

"You've never spoken in expressions before," said the car keys. "I'm not sure I like this."

"Well, we all have things we have to get used to," replied the wallet.

13

"I'm not normally one to succumb to petty jealousy," said the stove, "but are you going to cook every meal in that thing from now on?"

"It is easy to use," said Albert.

"I am a finely tuned food preparation device capable of producing an almost limitless variation of dishes," explained the slow cooker.

"Well tonight you're just heating up beans and some meat," replied the stove. "So don't be so impressed with yourself."

"Not just meat and beans," Albert said. "A culinary delight of the Midwest." It had been raining most of the day, so Albert had spent the day working on the travel book and trying to cook using Harvey's chili recipe.

"I'm not sure that I would classify…" replied the stove until they were interrupted by a knock at the door.

Albert pushed back his chair and stood up. "I'm not expecting anyone," he said. "Maybe it wasn't the door." He paused a moment to listen. The knock came again, this time louder.

"That's definitely the door," said the cell phone.

Albert left the kitchen and went to the front door. He peaked through the small decorative window at the top and saw his brother standing on the front step. Albert unlocked and opened the door.

"Hello Albert," said his brother.

"Hello," said Albert. He couldn't remember the last time his brother came to the house. In fact, he couldn't remember meeting with his brother anywhere but a restaurant, store or park.

"Can I come in?" asked his brother.

"Of course," replied Albert. He moved backward and swung the door open wider so that his brother could come into the house. "Do you want to come and sit in the kitchen? I was just cooking some dinner."

"Okay," said his brother. "That actually smells good. What is it?"

"I'm trying out a friend's chili recipe," said Albert.

"A friend?" asked his brother. "You've never talked about a friend before."

"I met him on the trip," Albert replied.

He led his brother into the kitchen and they sat down at the table. Albert could see he was wearing the watch.

"I see you still have that monstrous thing," said his brother glancing at the motor coach parked outside the kitchen window.

"Yes," said Albert. "I'm buying it from the manufacturer. I sent back the signed paperwork today as a matter of fact."

"So you'll be taking other trips then?" asked his brother.

"Yes," said Albert. "I like traveling and the motor coach is like taking a bit of home with you."

"You sound like the brochure," said his brother. "But I suppose it is." They were both silent for a short time.

"I'm sorry about the other day," said his brother finally.

"That's okay," said Albert. "I'm glad we talked about it."

"I am too," said his brother. "I wasn't at first, but after awhile I was okay." He was quiet for few moments and then continued. "Did you really come across a bear in the woods?" he asked.

"Yes," said Albert. "A mother and two cubs. I just stood still and she eventually left."

"And how long were you lost in the woods?" asked his brother.

"A couple of days," said Albert. "But I had the motor coach and plenty of food and water. Once I figured out my location, it was easy to find my way out."

"And you weren't scared?" asked his brother.

"I was completely scared," said Albert. "Especially when I was lost."

"Oh," said his brother.

"I'm writing about all of it in a travel book," explained Albert.

He picked up a copy of the travel manuscript he'd been marking up and handed it to his brother. At first his brother only leafed through it. Then he began to read more thoroughly. After a couple of pages he stopped and restarted reading it from the first page.

While his brother read, Albert set the table and served them chili from the slow cooker. His brother continued to read as he ate, hardly looking at the bowl. He simply spooned the food into his mouth as he went through page after page of the manuscript.

After they finished their chili, Albert cleared the table and put on a pot of coffee. His brother stayed focused on the manuscript. Albert poured them both a cup of coffee and put out a plate of cookies. They had drank most of the coffee and ate half the plate of cookies when his brother turned over the last page.

Albert looked at him expectantly. His brother sat back in his chair and tapped his chin. It was a habit Albert had watched him do ever since they were children. He looked up at Albert and smiled.

"This is very good," said his brother.

Albert smiled back. "You really like it?" he asked.

"I do Albert," said his brother. "And I think I understand what the trip was like for you."

"A lot of it was hard," said Albert. "But I also enjoyed it."

"I can tell that from your writing," said his brother gesturing towards the manuscript. "I don't know a lot about writing, but I think that's what good writing does." Then he added, "I'm proud of you, Albert."

14

"I think we're almost there," said the editor. "You'll need to add more details to a couple of these sections and I think you should move that one story up further."

"Yes," agreed Albert. He'd been taking notes as he and the editor went through the manuscript. For the first time since they'd started working together, Albert was meeting with him in his office.

Albert pointed to a photo on the desk. "Is this your family?" he asked.

"It is," said the editor. "That's my wife Ellen and our children Mark and Susanna. You're not married, right?"

"No," replied Albert. "No children either. I have a brother and two nieces."

"Do you see them often?" asked the editor.

"Actually no," said Albert.

"Do they live far away?" asked the editor.

"Not terribly," said Albert. "I see my brother about once a month."

"You know," said the editor. "We've never talked about anything but work before."

Albert considered this and realized the editor was correct. Throughout all the years they worked together there was never a conversation that wasn't about an manual or a client. Albert felt a pang of regret.

"I'm sorry about that," he said.

"No worries," said the editor. "It's never really too late to get to know someone, is it?"

"I suppose not," said Albert. This made him feel a bit better. "I should really go to see my nieces more often too."

"How old are they?" asked the editor.

"I think they're eight and ten," said Albert.

"That's a fun age," said the editor. "Childhood goes by fast. If you don't stay on top of it, you'll miss it. And just remember, as an uncle you get to do something your brother doesn't."

"What's that?" asked Albert.

"Go home afterward," said the editor. Albert was puzzled at first, then he realized that the editor was making a joke. Albert let out a brief snort.

"That's why I don't edit humor," explained the editor.

"That was another joke," said Albert.

"Yes," said the editor. He looked at his watch. "It's past noon…what do you say we grab some lunch?"

"Sure," said Albert.

"Great," said the editor. "And let's agree to not talk about business while we eat. We'll just get to know each other better."

Albert nodded. It occurred to him that talking to people quickly became sort of a habit. The more he did it, the more he liked it.

15

"It was a nice trip," said the bicycle, "but I have to admit I'm glad to be off of that rack on the back of the motor coach. I never thought I'd miss my hooks."

"I guess it was a rough ride for you back there," said Albert. He was retrieving a few items from the garage.

"The change of scenery did me good, though," said the bicycle. "I believe I am a hybrid model."

"And the campground roads weren't that bad," said Albert.

"Yes," said the bicycle. "It's a nice day. How about a ride?"

Albert looked back at the motor coach. "I don't have a lot of time," he said. "I haven't been through my checklists yet."

"It'll keep," said the bicycle. "The weather might not."

Albert considered the offer. "Okay," he said finally. "Let's see if there's been any changes around the neighborhood."

Albert lifted the bicycle off the hooks and set it on the floor of the driveway. "There are few bugs on your frame," he said. "I'll get the hose."

"We can worry about it when we get back," said the bicycle. "A few stains aren't going to hurt me."

Albert got on the bicycle and rode it down the driveway and into the street. Just before reaching the corner he passed two people sitting on their front porch. Albert waved to them and they waved back at him.

A few minutes later he saw a parent helping a child to ride their own bike. "Hello," said Albert.

"Hello," the parent said back. The child smiled and waved. "Nice day for a ride," said the parent.

"Yes," said Albert. "It is."

Not long afterward Albert suggested, "Maybe we'll ride downtown."

"That sounds like a good idea," agreed the bicycle. "You can get a water. You forgot to fill your bottle before we left."

Albert nodded. He made a few turns and before long they were in the downtown area, surrounded by a number of people. Albert exchanged greetings with most of them as he passed them.

He pulled the bicycle into the rack in front of the bakery so he could get off and purchase a water. Inside the baker was busy but told Albert he was anxious to hear about the trip. He suggested he stop by another day. Albert agreed and walked back out to the bicycle.

"Ready to head back home?" asked Albert. "I have to leave soon."

"Yes," said the bicycle. "As far as you ride, that's how far you need to ride back."

"That is true," said Albert.

Back at the house, Albert placed the bike on the rack at the rear of the motor coach. "I know you like your hooks," he said.

"That's okay," replied the bicycle. "At least I have a good view from here."

Albert nodded and walked to the front of the motor coach. Once inside, he went through his usual checklists. The gauges were all correct – including the fuel, oil and temperature. There were no warning such as transmission or tire pressure. The batteries were charged and the fresh water tank was filled. He tapped the center display to check on the navigation system. His destination was set and the first instructions were on the screen.

"I think it's a good idea if you use the navigation throughout the trip," suggested the wallet. "You've had enough personal growth experiences in the woods for awhile."

"Was that another joke?" asked the car keys.

"As a matter of fact it was," said the wallet.

"That makes three this month," said the car keys. "But who's counting."

"Apparently you are," said the cell phone.

Albert took a final look around the cab for any signs of trouble and turned the key to start the motor coach. He turned the headlights on and off. Then he turned on each turn signal and finally the hazard lights.

"Let's just get this show on the road," said the car keys.

"Not yet," said the reading glasses.

Albert glanced in the mirror to his left, then the mirror to his right. He tapped the display screen again and checked the rear view camera. The passenger side door opened and his brother got into the motor coach and sat down.

"Sorry I'm late," he said. "I had to finish a few things before the weekend."

"That's okay," said Albert.

"By the way," said his brother, "I checked during my walk up the driveway and all of your lights are working. I also checked your exhaust for leaks and made sure all of the outside compartments were secured."

"Thank you," said Albert. "It's much easier to check the lights with two people." He pulled the seatbelt across his lap and clicked it in place. His brother did the same.

"Ready?" asked Albert.

"Not completely," said his brother. "But I think I'll be okay. This is just a long weekend, right?"

"Yes," said Albert.

"No bears…no getting lost in the woods…no bocce?" continued his brother.

"Definitely no bears or getting lost in the woods," said Albert. "I'm not sure if there will be bocce or not."

"Well I'm not playing if there is," said his brother.

"That's okay," said Albert.

"In that case I think I'm ready," said his brother.

Albert put the motor coach in gear and maneuvered the vehicle into the street. He turned left at the edge of the driveway and in a few moments was on the highway.

"Thank you Albert," said his brother.

"For what?" asked Albert.

"Just thank you," said his brother. Albert nodded at his brother and smiled. Albert knew he wasn't going to stop talking to things. He just figured he would spend more time talking to people.

Talks to Things
By Dominic R. Villari

Other books by Dominic R. Villari:

Fiction and Non-fiction
The Ginger Bread Man
Practical Storytelling

Children's Books
The Cat of La Mancha – Don Quixote for Kids
You Have to Wear Pants!
Tan's Tile – A Tale of Creative Thought
The Way Forward
Don't Poke the Bear

For more information, visit:
Figment Press
www.figmentpress.com